THE

COLOR OF ABSENCE

—————•—————

12 STORIES

ABOUT LOSS AND HOPE

THE
COLOR OF ABSENCE

———•———

12 STORIES

ABOUT LOSS AND HOPE

EDITED BY JAMES HOWE

SIMON PULSE
New York London Toronto Sydney Singapore

First Simon Pulse edition January 2003

Compilation and introduction copyright © 2001 by James Howe

"Summer of Love" copyright © 2001 by Annette Curtis Klause • "What Are You Good At?" copyright © 2001 by Roderick Townley • "Atomic Blue Pieces" copyright © 2001 by Angela Johnson • "The Tin Butterfly" copyright © 2001 by Norma Fox Mazer • "The Fire Pond" copyright © 2001 by Michael J. Rosen • "Chair: A Story for Voices" copyright © 2001 by Virginia Euwer Wolff • "Red Seven" copyright © 2001 by C. B. Christiansen • "Shoofly Pie" copyright © 2001 by Naomi Shihab Nye • "You're Not a Winner Unless Your Picture's in the Paper" copyright © 2001 by Avi • "Season's End" copyright © 2001 by Walter Dean Myers • "The Rialto" copyright © 2001 by Jacqueline Woodson and Chris Lynch • "Enchanted Night" copyright © 2001 by James Howe

SIMON PULSE
An imprint of Simon & Schuster Children's Publishing Division
1230 Avenue of the Americas, New York, NY 10020

All rights reserved, including the right of reproduction in whole or in part in any form.

Also available in an Atheneum Books for Young Readers hardcover edition.
Designed by Ann Bobco
The text of this book was set in Janson Text.

Printed in the United States of America
4 6 8 10 9 7 5 3

The Library of Congress has cataloged the hardcover edition as follows:
Color of absence / edited by James Howe.
p.   cm.
Summary: A collection of stories dealing with different kinds of loss experience by young people.
ISBN 0-689-82862-4 (hc)
1. Grief—Juvenile fiction. 2. Short stories, American. [1. Grief—Fiction. 2. Short stories.]
I. Howe, James, 1946–
PZ5.L773 2001
[Fic]—dc21   00-044206

ISBN 0-689-85667-9 (pbk.)

CONTENTS

CONTENTS

For those we have lost
—J. H.

INTRODUCTION

While reading Annette Curtis Klause's young adult novel *The Silver Kiss*, I was struck by this sentence: "The tears that prickled his eyes broke his bonds, and he fled, while she sat and cried for all things lost."

The truth of crying for "all things lost" gave resonance to an idea I'd had for some time, that of editing a collection of short stories on the theme of loss. I knew I wanted these stories to be for young adults, because in adolescence we feel our losses as if for the first time, with a greater depth of pain and drama than we are aware of having experienced ever before. In reality, by the time we reach our teen years, we've already experienced many losses in our lives. Perhaps what we are feeling—for the first time—is an awareness of an accumulation of losses, an understanding that we will experience loss again and again in our lives, coming to know it as an inevitable part of the human condition.

And so with each loss, we come to cry for every loss. Crying for a lost friend, we cry for a loss of innocence as well, for the belief that friendship is forever, that love will endure. When we mourn a death, we mourn our own mortality. And with each step we take toward adulthood, we let go of the children we once were and will never be again.

The stories in this collection reflect this notion that each loss contains all losses. While the individual stories focus on different forms of loss—the death of a parent or grandparent or pet, the disappearance of a sibling or friend, the end of a relationship, the fading away of a loved one because of disease or age—all are shadowed by the accumulation of losses in the characters' lives. "Mama cries all the time now," Angela Johnson writes in "Atomic Blue Pieces," "but I don't really think she's crying for Leon. I think she's crying for all the ones who have left her." Norma Fox Mazer expresses a similar sentiment in her story, "The Tin Butterfly": "And just for a moment she understood it all—how loss comes to everyone. How it was a part of life, like the leaves coming off the trees in autumn and the snow melting in the spring."

A recognition that loss is part of the human condition enables us ultimately to accept not only the losses we are dealt, but the absences that become entwined in the fabric of our lives. As I read through all the stories in this collection, I found that what they had in common was the idea that loss means *change*. With a loss of the familiar comes a loss of a sense of self. "Who am I now?" is more on the characters' minds than "Why is this happening?"

> *Your absence has gone through me*
> *Like thread through a needle*
> *Everything I do is stitched with its color.*

• • •

These lines, from a poem by W.S. Merwin, are quoted in "The Rialto," by Jacqueline Woodson and Chris Lynch. Jacqueline Woodson goes on to say in the voice of her character, Caryn, "And I read the words over and over again imagining the color of absence . . ." How eloquently this expresses the notion that our lives are forever changed by the losses we endure. I am indebted to Jacqueline for the title of this book. Once again, it is another writer's words that crystallized my own thoughts.

I feel extremely fortunate to have gathered this extraordinary group of writers together in one volume. I am proud to be among them with a story of my own. The stories you will find in these pages are deep and personal, sad and funny, touching and universally true. They reflect despair and they offer hope. In shifting the realities of their characters' lives, the authors give their characters—and their readers—the chance to look back, to look within, and ultimately to look ahead, as they begin the task of stitching new lives where the thread of absence is but one color among many.

—James Howe

T H E

COLOR OF ABSENCE

———————•———————

12 STORIES

ABOUT LOSS AND HOPE

SUMMER OF LOVE

ANNETTE CURTIS KLAUSE

I t was the summer of 1967, the Summer of Love, the newspapers called it, and I wandered the streets of San Francisco with the most plentiful source of food around me since the day I'd died. Runaways from all over the country were lured here by the dream of freely offered sex, plentiful drugs, and rock 'n' roll on every corner; and layered over the gray, workaday city was a multi-colored party that seemed to exist in a parallel world. I walked that world.

I was almost a happy man, if a three-hundred-year-old vampire could ever be called happy. This is what I call fast food, I thought. These children knew no fear. Strangers were their friends. All they needed was love. They slept in doorways, in the parks, and in "liberated houses" that held dozens. How easy it was to slip in next to a girl drunk on cheap wine and take my own wine from her rich, young veins. It was fortunate that the drugs they imbibed had no effect on me, else I'd have been staggering around half-blind all the time. But my unnatural body screened all chemicals out that didn't nurture it, and in these good times I pissed a red stream of waste maybe twice a week.

Love, love, love. How meaningless it was to me. My own loved ones were centuries dead, and I, forever trapped in-between, frozen in the form of a youth not yet twenty. What did I care of love? The ones I'd loved had always abandoned me or betrayed me. I wouldn't be what I am except for one I loved. Yet, in this city of love, I could go anywhere—join in parties, hang out at those spontaneous park festivals called be-ins, wander nighttime concerts—and all welcomed me. If I didn't tell my name, no one pressed me; if I lied, no one cared. I had friends everywhere, and still no one knew who I was. "Who's that pale dude?" I'd hear a boy say as I watched my menu sway to the music, the colored lights dancing on their faces. "What's the name of that cute blond?" a girl would whisper to her friend, winding her fingers in the layers of beads around her neck as if they were in my hair. But they never found out, not even when I sweet-talked one of those yearning girls out under the stars and lulled her into a sparkling silver trance of ecstasy, my fangs firmly planted in her neck. I was gentle with them, let there be no mistake in that, and I tried very hard to leave a drop of life in their veins so they would see the dawn, but I could not make friends with those I hunted—the thought repelled me. I didn't take the pills they gave me, and I turned down the weed they offered in hand-rolled, smoldering cigarettes. "I prefer to drink," I'd explain if I had to.

But I loved the music. Wild and free, tunes went on and on, meandering out to the moon and beyond. I danced to the throbbing music by myself, arms waving, eyes closed, and pretended to be moved by life. I floated through the laughter, music, and excitement of the night in a dark bubble of my own making, and it was cold inside, very cold, but the less that was known of me, the safer I was. In my stolen bell-bottom jeans and flowered shirts, I looked just like them but I never would be, and I doubted that their precious, shallow love would save me if they knew.

In the day, I had to have my sleep, and in an alley behind a row of shabby Victorian houses, I'd found my den—an abandoned garage with crumbled gingerbread trim. Perhaps it was a stable once. I covered the windows with old blankets I stole from revelers in the park, and stuffed the chinks in the wood with newspaper to keep out the damaging light. Under the floorboards beneath my bed I kept a suitcase with all that was valuable to me: a meager portion of my native soil, without which I could not sleep, and a painted portrait of those I once held dear. I curled above that suitcase every day, in a deep, sodden coma, too full of rich human blood to bother with the rats that shared my home.

It was there, one misty morning, groggy with the need to sleep off excess, that I found the cat.

It must have squeezed under the ill-fitting doors looking for shelter from the damp night air. Woken by my return, it crouched on my pile of blankets in a dusty corner behind a stack of old tires and stared warily at me.

"Lucky for you I've had my dinner, tabby," I said. "Now off with you."

It should have been scared, animals ran from me, but instead it hissed.

Somehow, the absurdity made me laugh.

My laughter made it crouch lower, and its ears flattened. It edged away, and I saw how skinny it was and weak. For a second I remembered crawling in the forest newly made, starving, and too stunned to know that blood was now my food. Just then, one of the occasional rats chose to make an ill-advised dash across the floor. I don't know why I did it, curiosity perhaps, but I snatched the squealing rat up. I tore the creature open with my teeth and tossed it near the cat. The cat flinched but didn't run.

"Well, there you are, puss," I said. "Food with your lodging. What are you waiting for?"

Slowly it crept from the shadows and finally sniffed the corpse. I could see then it was female. It didn't take her long to recognize a meal, and she wolfed the rat meat down so fast, I feared she would vomit.

"Steady on," I warned. "I don't care to share my den with cat puke."

When she'd finished I flung the remnants under the door and stuffed the crack with an old coat. Ignoring the cat, I sank to my bed and took my crimson sleep.

The cat shot out the door the next evening as soon as it was opened, not surprising, as she had managed to spend the entire night without soiling the floor. I didn't expect to see her again.

I was wrong. She was there in the jingle-jangle morning I'd heard the band sing of the night before. She sat by my front door with an expectant look on her little tabby face. What could I do? I found her another rat.

The routine became a habit. Dawn. Cat. Rat. Then she slept in a corner of my den. "But don't get used to it," I told her. "I'll be moving on soon."

Perhaps because I spent all my time avoiding conversation with humans, I soon found myself confiding in the cat. I only shared a few words at first. "Good morning," I'd say. "Found a plump brunette at the Quicksilver concert. How was your night?" Soon I surrendered more details. "Last night's girlfriend was an Airplane fan," I might begin. "I thought she'd give in easily, but she'd traded her brains for LSD, and my charms didn't work on her. She screamed when I bit her and I'm afraid I overreacted. I was really sorry afterward, cat. Honestly. I had to drop her in the bay so no one would find her."

It was such a relief to confess.

The cat was wary at first. She wanted the meat, but she kept her distance, eyeing me suspiciously as if trying to place what kind of creature I was. Perhaps I smelled of death; perhaps I smelled of nothing known to her. Her aloofness saddened me. Was my only intimacy with those who lived to be when draining the very source of that life? A foolish question, for I knew that to be true. Nevertheless, I made a game of befriending her.

My words brought her near, yet she was shy of my touch. She ducked from my first advances, and danced on the shadow tip of my embrace, but I didn't give up. I wooed her like a lover. Each day she lingered longer within reach, and I held myself in check. Each day her little ribs became less obvious, and she trembled less. I remember the electric crackle of joy the first time she let me stroke her head.

Soon, like a fool, I named the beast. Grimalkin, I called her—a witch's cat's name, but I'm close enough to a witch in most minds, I suppose. Stroking her became my delight—and hers. I had forgotten how a purr could buzz in one's fingers like summer. She slept at the foot of my bed.

One morning I came home to find a mouse upon my pillow. "And now you are the provider?" I asked her as she wound between my legs. The bursting fullness in my chest was fleeting, but frightened me. I readied for sleep briskly, paying her no more heed. When I woke in the evening, I found her curled against my stomach. "Why?" I asked. "You will find no warmth there." But the fullness was back and wouldn't be ignored. It was I who took warmth from her.

The summer danced on, the music played, and the generous girls came and went. I tried to be careful, I truly did, but excess was all around, and I became prey to it, too. I had spent almost three hundred years in trying to control the lust, I had even tried to exist on the blood of beasts alone, and now one hedonistic summer had undone me. I found it harder and harder to stop in time. If I took too much, at least they died gently, I consoled myself, at least they felt no pain. I refused to feed on their terror like others of my kind, but feed I must, so under an August moon I romanced a girl, all fringes and swirling skirts, that I'd lured out from the bands and the smoky air of the dance hall called the Filmore.

"What's your favorite band?" she asked.

"The Grateful Dead," I answered. Christ, I was almost getting a sense of humor.

"I'm not a runaway," she told me when I asked. "I live in Mountain View with my mom, and sister, and three old cats."

"I have a cat, too," I said, surprising myself.

I soon was sorry. My admission provoked an avalanche of anecdotes. "Enough!" I said, finally losing patience, and drew her to me, my gaze on her neck, my gums itching.

"Ooh! You remind me of that Doors singer, Jim Morrison," she said. "Beautiful and scary at the same time."

I decided she was more intelligent than most. "You are beautiful, too," I whispered, trailing my fingers down her cheek, capturing her eyes with mine.

She relaxed into my arms, surrendering to the spell I wove, and I took her throat. "The stars are swirling," she said vaguely as I sipped gently on her blood. "Did you give me some drugs or something?" She giggled weakly. "But I'd remember, wouldn't . . ." Her voice trailed off into a sigh. I allowed myself to tumble into the lake of dreams with her, drowning, drowning in the sweet froth of her life, and I would have finished her in that glorious haze, drained her of the nectar that sustained me, except I remembered the three old cats, and all of a sudden I couldn't go on. Ashamed, I left her there in Golden Gate Park to wake with the dawn and wonder if someone had slipped some acid in her drink.

Grimalkin wasn't waiting at the garage door. After half a summer of the same routine, she wasn't there. I tried to shrug off the disappointment. It had to happen sooner or later—either she would leave or I would. Maybe she was delayed by a mouse, I told myself, but not believing it. I hesitated over whether to block the crack under the door, but common sense won out and I grabbed for the dusty old coat. A day out won't harm her, I thought, but a touch of sunlight would certainly harm me.

She was already curled on my bed.

"Grimalkin! Trickster!" I exclaimed. The joy of seeing her surprised me into laughter. Who would have thought? I made ready for bed hastily with a smile on my face.

When I woke in the evening, she was still in the same spot. "Wake up, lazybones," I said over my shoulder, but her only response was a slight opening of her eyelids.

"What ails you, puss?" I asked, rolling over to stroke her. She trembled. "Ah, yes, I'm very cold," I said, making it a joke. Then I noticed the slime around her mouth and found it was possible to be colder still.

I smelled a rankness in the air I hadn't noticed in the morning. Before I identified the source, Grimalkin showed me. She wobbled to her feet, staggered a few steps, and vomited on my blanket. She collapsed again and lay there panting.

I panicked.

I, who had lived by my wits for centuries and could mesmerize or crush with my strength; I, who could fly with wings through the night, or drift like mist; I, who thought I was above the laws of nature, didn't know what to do for a little sick cat.

I swept her into my arms and took to the streets. I had no money and didn't know where to go. I would have to ask for help. Did these people who danced all night and had no job I knew of have doctors who healed for the sake of love? If anyone knew it would be in Haight-Ashbury, the kaleidoscope heart of the alternate city.

I ran to a head shop on Haight, which I knew was open until midnight. Wrinkling my nose against the overwhelming stench of incense and patchouli oil, I pushed past the browsers around the comic book racks and the bulletin board, to the far end of a glass display case full of pipes, roach clips, and other drug paraphernalia. The girl at the counter was almost hidden by racks dripping with multicolored scarves and beads.

"Where do the sick go?" I asked her urgently.

She stared at me blankly for a moment, and I would have grabbed her if my arms were not full.

"The free clinic, man." I turned to see a young man with a bushy black beard, holding a flyer up for me to read the address.

"The doctors volunteer," he said. "It's for the street kids who don't have money."

I thanked him and hurried out.

"Stay cool!" I heard him call after me—advice or a meaningless salute, I don't know.

The clinic was in the basement of a church. That stopped me cold. I stood there staring at the looming facade, a sinking feeling in my gut. I must have held my cat too tight. She squeaked in pain. That decided me. But as soon as I crossed the threshold I felt my insides crush together in fear.

A motley assortment of young people sat in the rows of ancient straight-backed wooden chairs, or lounged in the few tattered armchairs that sat on the cloudy linoleum floor.

"Dude's got a cat," a youth in a purple shirt said to no one in particular, and giggled irrelevantly.

A shivering boy with large black pupils was led past me by his friends. Too much LSD or mescaline, I guessed. "You'll be safe here," I heard one friend say. "They'll give you something to bring you down."

"They never call the police," said the other.

The girl at the table looked over her square, pink-lensed glasses at me. "Whatcha here for?" she asked, pen hovering ready over a printed form.

I held out Grimalkin.

"Cat sick?" she asked, the space between her eyebrows creasing with concern.

I nodded, still unable to speak.

"Bummer," she said. "I dunno, tho'. We don't do pets."

I folded Grimalkin back to my chest, and swallowed a scream. The weight of the crucifix somewhere over my head seemed to bear down on me and take away my thoughts. I didn't know the question to ask next.

The girl did, however. "Jerry," she called through a door to her right. "Where do we send people with cats?"

A tall young man in a white coat over jeans and T-shirt

poked his head through the door. He looked me over and winced. "You sure it's not you that needs the help?" he asked.

I shook my head.

He sighed and came over. "Hi, baby," he said to Grimalkin, gently stroking her head. "It's okay, it's just Dr. Jerry. I've got two like you at home."

Unlike so many, he then looked me in the eyes. I saw compassion there and, for a moment, it took the weight from my chest.

"Listen . . . uh . . . sorry, what's your name?" he asked.

"Simon," I answered before I could help it.

"Simon," he repeated, and I felt a slight shock as someone spoke my true name to me for the first time in years. "I don't know anything about sick animals. I don't even know what the normal heart rate of a cat is, but I know a vet," he said, "a friend. She lives near. I'll call her. Maybe she'll come over."

I waited in that clammy basement, stroking my cat, overhearing words like *clap*, *knocked up*, *bad trip*, and *pain*. Someone cried loudly in another room for a while. Patients went in the back, emerged again, and left. Others came in from the street to take their places.

"You'll be better, 'Malkin," I whispered to my cat over and over. "You'll be fine, little queen." I warned away the talkative with venom in my eyes.

A black woman in a long print dress came through the front door. She wore bangles and short, sculpted hair like a fine, dark dandelion. She scanned the room, then approached me purposefully. Why me? I wanted to flee, but it was too important to stay.

"I'm Avis," she said, sitting down beside me. "Jerry called me about your cat. Let me see."

This was the vet, then. Reluctantly I let her take Grimalkin on her lap as the skin on my back twitched from the scrutiny of the bored and curious. The cat lay limply in a hammock of bright fabric as Avis prodded and probed. The vet lifted Grimalkin's lips and studied her gums.

"I'm afraid you have a really sick kitty," Avis finally said.

I know that, I thought angrily. I know that. But the words wouldn't leave my lips.

The vet patted my knee as if she read my thoughts and understood. "Her kidneys are enlarged," Avis continued. "And she's in shock. My best guess is that she's been poisoned."

I rose to my feet faster than a mortal, ready to kill whoever would dare, and the vet cringed, surprise and fear on her face.

"N-not on purpose," she stammered. "Something she found. Like antifreeze. It's sweet, cats like it, but it causes permanent damage."

Antifreeze. I thought of the cans I'd moved to a corner of my den when I first took possession. It was possible. Why the hell hadn't I thrown them away?

A tremor passed through Grimalkin's body, and the cat let out a yowl, causing me to drop to my knees. Avis let me reclaim her. "I'm sorry. I think she's dying of kidney failure," the vet said gently as I buried my face in Grimalkin's fur.

"There's nothing you can do?" I asked, raising hopeless eyes, already knowing the answer.

Avis shook her head. "It's best now to put her out of her pain. I can take care of it if you like—no charge."

"No!" I cried. And I ran from there, ran all the way home.

Back in my den, I held Grimalkin in my arms. She was alternately stiff, then limp, racked by tremors.

I couldn't save her, and I couldn't turn her into one such as me, even if I wanted to; there was only one thing I could give her—peace.

I had calmed wild animals in my time—soothed them a little so I could feed—but I had never turned my full power to mesmerize upon a beast. I wasn't even sure I could. But now was the time to try. I could lull her to sleep slowly and peacefully, lure her into gentle dreams and let her go to a place where I could never follow. Trapped in this world, I would never walk a long, white tunnel and find her waiting. I would live centuries more and never see her again. At least her blood would make her part of me. A mote of her would live in me awhile.

It hurt to unsheathe my fangs—it had never hurt before.

I held her close, and rocked her, and whispered love until I heard a tiny purr. "Brave girl," I said. "Brave, brave, sweet girl." Then I bent my head as if in prayer.

I didn't mind the fur in my mouth, it was precious to me, but the first taste of blood nearly choked me. I carried on, anyway, and wove the spell. It didn't take long. She relaxed against me, she kneaded my chest, for a moment her purr grew large, and then it was gone. The blood ceased to flow, and she was but a shell.

13

I didn't know that I could cry.

It was time to move on, I knew that now. I had to go far from this place that had seduced me. If not for a little cat, I would have become the demon I had fought so long not to be. But she had ruined me. No matter where I went, I would yearn for love now I remembered what it was, and where would anyone such as I find love again?

From the Author

"I don't think I have a story," I told Jim Howe over the phone when he first invited me to contribute to this anthology. I didn't have one already written on the theme of loss, and I didn't know if I had time to write one—my mind was much too full with a novel that I was trying to coax into existence. As much as I was thrilled to be asked, I seriously didn't think I could do it. Then the follow-up letter came, and in it he quoted a line from my novel The Silver Kiss *and eloquently placed it in context with loss as part of the human condition. Well, that puts the pressure on, doesn't it? One* has *to contribute to an anthology when something one wrote is given as an example of universal truth—the sneaky devil. But I didn't have a story.*

The next morning I was staring out the window after a late breakfast, procrastinating as usual, drinking an extra cup of coffee, daydreaming, anything rather than get on with the day's chores. Loss, I thought. The most recent loss in my mind was that of our cat, Mr. Tumnus, to cancer. No matter how many times you lose a loved pet, it never becomes easier. He'd put up a successful fight for a year, but

15

the cancer came back worse than ever, and my husband and I had to make that terrible, final decision. One death seems to make all the others fresh again in memory.
The Silver Kiss *was also fresh in my mind because of that letter. Did Simon, my vampire, ever have a cat? I wondered, almost jokingly.*

That's when my brain took off.

Maybe he did. When was it? What happened? Ideas came fast and furious, all mixed up with my own still-aching grief.

I'd better jot these ideas down for later, I thought, or I'll forget them. I ran upstairs to my computer to create a file and toss in those notes—five hours later I had a story, a story about someone I never thought I'd write about again, and a tribute to Mr. Tumnus, Stella, Siegfried, Tobette, Jenny, Wolfbane, Tobermory, and Zoë.

WHAT ARE YOU GOOD AT?

RODERICK TOWNLEY

I

You hear all this stuff. Remember on TV? There was this girl looking like a skeleton, she was talking to all those senators. It about made you sick.

But you can't go by that. When my dad called he sounded real normal. Said he wanted me to come up, stay with him on the unit. Mom said no, but when you got an old man like mine and he calls you, you go.

I never been to Kansas City before. I didn't have any money except twenty dollars my mom gave me, and the bus ticket so I wouldn't have to hitch. Which I would've and she knew it.

Good I had that ticket, with the rain coming down hard as it was. I got soaked anyway by the time I found the place. It looked like a hospital, except it wasn't, it was where you go after you already been to the hospital. The linoleum was shiny like it was made of oil, and there was a lady at the front desk, real nice. She called upstairs. Told me to put down my grip and sit tight, it'd be a few minutes. Which I did.

That was the longest ten minutes I ever sat. I pulled out an Almond Joy. It was crushed from being in my wet pocket. I was telling myself not to expect him to look like I remembered from five years ago. I kept thinking about that girl on the TV.

Finally a door opens down the hall and this nurse comes toward me. She's pretty, I guess, blonde hair and nice, but tired around the eyes, the way Mom gets sometimes, only younger.

"You John Beener's boy?" she says, and I say yeah and she stands and looks at me. "You sure are, aren't you? Look just like him." Her name's Betty, she says, and she shakes my hand and takes me up.

It's a small place, just a little hallway with rooms on both sides and a lounge at the end. I went behind her. There was a smell I couldn't tell what it was. One smell under another, like pee and Clorox. That Almond Joy wasn't setting so well, I should've chewed it more. She got to the lounge and said, "John, somebody to see you."

There he was, setting by himself at the table. The TV was on and somebody in hospital pajamas was watching it in a wheelchair, not paying attention. But my old man, I'll tell you, he looked good. Same old horse face and scraggy mustache, same black eyes that know all about you before you say anything. And he wasn't wearing hospital stuff. He had a black silk shirt on and sharp-looking jeans. Even his boots was polished.

"Cooter?" he says.

"Hi, Dad."

He smiles that great, crooked-tooth smile of his. "Come over here." He reached out and grabbed my arm and pulled himself up. "You're wet as a muskrat."

He gave me a hug, wet as I was. "Smell like one, too," he said, which made me laugh. He smelled like after-shave and cigarettes. "Sit down," he said, and we sat, looking at each other. "Goddamn," he said.

"You look great, Dad."

He asked me lots of stuff about how I found my way up from Arkansas and how Mom was and whether I still went fishing like we used to when he was living with us.

He tapped on his shirt pocket, then stuck a couple of fingers in without looking and pulled out a Winston. He snapped open a lighter and lit up and put the lighter away all in one motion.

"So," he said, "what are you good at?"

"Good at? Fishing, I guess. And cards."

"Kind of cards?"

"Solitaire."

"You won't get rich playing solitaire. Know any poker?"

"Some."

"I'll teach you. You need to know a trade. Look in that drawer over there."

I looked in the chest where the coffeemaker was setting and a basket of plastic spoons and Sweet'n Low. I found a mess of cards, like from five decks all mixed together.

"That my sweetheart?" he sang out. A colored nurse was coming in with trays.

"How you doin' today, you sweet thing?" She gave his head a playful push.

"Donna," he said, "I want you to meet my boy, Cooter."

19

"John, watch your ashes. Hi, Cooter." Donna nudged the tin ashtray under his cigarette. "You know, you're going to have to put that thing out. Harry'll bite your head off if he smells cigarettes while he's trying to eat."

"Cooter's staying with me a few days, isn't that right, Coot?"

"Sure is, Dad."

That stopped Donna. "What, on the unit?"

"We're going to have a hell of a time."

Donna looked over at Betty, who'd just come in.

"Did you hear that, Betty?"

"It's okay, John's got an extra bed in his room."

"Has anybody cleared this?"

"No, and nobody's going to." Betty turned the guy in the wheelchair around and pushed him up to the table. "Time to eat, Rob."

Rob looked like what I seen from pictures. Like that girl on TV. He was a skeleton with a scowl. Not really a scowl, I guess. He didn't have enough expression for it.

"Better put it out, John," said Betty. "People are coming in."

"Okay, Beautiful." He stubbed it.

Donna was carrying in trays and she put one in front of me, too. I couldn't make out what it was, stew or something. And there was custard for dessert. I hadn't eaten but that Almond Joy since last night. It looked like nobody was going to say grace, so I just said a quick Thank-you-oh-Lord under my breath and dug in.

"Hey, Coot, can you get me a Coke from the nurse's station?"

"Sure, Dad." I ran out to the little glassed-in booth

and Betty handed me two Cokes, one for me. I came back and set a can in front of Dad.

"Could you open it for me, son?"

"Sure." I popped the flip top and set it down. I saw his hand reaching for it and not finding it.

"Can you put it in my hand?"

I just stared at him. I felt my eyes get hot, I couldn't help it. Damn, why didn't he *tell* me?

"Sure, Dad." I put the Coke in his hand, watching his eyes real close to see if he was fooling.

He drank a long gulp. "Ahh."

I looked up and there was this old guy standing in the doorway, holding onto a contraption on a metal pole. He spooked me for a second. His face was bumpy, like he had big boils all over him. I thought of that story of Job our minister tells. Smitten with boils. Especially with him in his bathrobe and holding that pole, he really could've been from the Bible. Not one of the nice parts.

"That you, Harry?" Dad called out.

The old guy shuffled in and felt for the seat next to me. I saw he was attached to a machine through a tube of some kind. Donna was telling him, this is the meat at twelve o'clock, there's the potatoes at four o'clock, and the dessert's at nine o'clock.

My God, I thought, two blind guys and a mute. And one of them happens to be my old man.

"You smoking again, John?" said the old guy.

"Caught me."

"Can you put it out? I can't eat with that."

"It's *been* out."

"Not very long."

"It's been out for hours, hasn't it Coot?"

"Who's that?" said Harry, looking around.

"Next to your elbow. My boy Charles. Is he good-looking or what?"

"You're John's boy?" He turned to me. I didn't really want his face that close. "Stand up against the light."

I looked to Dad for help, but he was just setting there grinning. I stood.

"You're getting big. Can't tell more than that. I've lost my eyes, same as your dad. He's been talking about you for weeks."

I sat down and he stuck out his hand and I had to shake it.

"When can I smoke?"

I looked around. It was the skeleton. He could talk.

Betty came by. "Rob, you know the times are posted right there on the wall."

"Where? I can't see that."

Harry let loose at him. "Well you know it's not when everybody's eating!"

Rob gave him a look of disgust and went back to picking at his vanilla custard. "This isn't a prison, you know."

"Hey Rob, I want you to say hello to my boy."

"I can smoke when I want."

"Rob," said my dad in his big voice. "My boy Cooter."

The skeleton looked over at me. "Can you take me downstairs so I can smoke?"

Betty came behind me and put her hands on my shoulders. "Not now, Rob. He's here to see his dad."

I liked that Betty.

"Let's go back to my room," Dad said. "I'll show you

where you're bunking." He reached down and picked up a cane that looked about as long as a fly rod, then pushed back his chair, latched onto my elbow, and steered me down the hall.

He turned on the radio, first thing, 61 Country, and had me go shut the door. He liked his music loud, always did. There was a guy dying across the hall, he said. I didn't know if I believed him, but maybe it was so. He still played his music like always, just with the door shut. The guy would have to die to the sounds of Diamond Rio.

Dad was taking tapes out of a cassette holder and putting them back, like he could tell which was which.

"I'm looking for my Travis Tritt. Can you find Travis Tritt?"

I started reading the names on the tapes. He had everybody you ever heard of, but I couldn't make out any order to it. It reminded me of the drawer of playing cards in the lounge.

"Those nurses been messing with my system again." He flipped off the radio and popped on the tape player, fast as a disc jockey. My dad, he's fast at everything. If anything got broke at home, he found a way to fix it.

"Hey Dad, remember that invention you made?"

"I have six inventions, son."

"The one that keeps the leaves out of the roof gutter?"

"Oh, that little baby's going to make us a pile of money. All's I need is fifty thousand and I can start production."

I looked at him, blind as he was, and I thought, if anybody could do it, he'd be the one.

Later, after dinner, he made good his promise to teach

me poker. He got Nurse Betty to sit down in the lounge while he whispered to me. "What you got, son? Don't let Betty hear."

Rob the skeleton shuffled by, taking little steps. He looked over Betty's shoulder, then gave her a disgusted look. "You think you can do better, Rob?" said Betty.

I whispered to Dad I only had two eights, but he acted real surprised. "Well, then, you better raise her. How *about* this kid!"

Betty gave him a straight look. "Don't you think I can see right through you, John Beener?" But when it came to put up or shut up, she folded, even though she was holding a pair of jacks. After a few hands, Betty owed me a dollar seventy-five, which she paid me, cash.

Later we sat back in the room and Dad taught me how to handle the cards so it looked like I knew what I was doing. Have you ever tried to shuffle with one hand? I practiced while he popped a George Johnson tape into the player.

Dad started singing along, dancing around the room while he took off his clothes for bed. He bumped into the bathroom door, which I'd left open, but he didn't mind. I'd forgot about that snake tattoo all down his left arm. The skin on his chest looked kind of brownish, with dark blotches on it. I looked away till he covered himself.

"You do any drugs, son?" he said, setting on the one chair next to the TV.

"Dad!"

"Just a question."

"Dad, I'm fourteen years old!"

He looked at me and I swear he could see me clear as

anything. "Son, at fourteen I was smoking marijuana. By twenty I was started on heroin."

I didn't think he should be telling me this stuff.

"I'm not saying the drugs wasn't good. The drugs was very good. But the drugs wasn't *that* good." He leaned back in the chair and stared at the ceiling. "Remember that."

"Is that how you got it, Dad?"

He kept staring at the white ceiling, which could've been black as tar as far as he knew.

"Yeah, it was."

There wasn't any sound for a while but the rain on the window.

"No damn needles. You promise?"

"Don't worry."

"That's a good answer. Your mom still working at the Piggly Wiggly?"

"She gave that up. I thought you knew."

"No, I didn't." He closed his eyes.

"Well," I said. I didn't know whether to leave out Buzzy or not, or whether Dad knew about him and Mom. "You know Tony Van Buskirk, Dad?"

His eyes stayed closed. "Don't guess I do."

"He's a friend of Mom's from the Piggly Wiggly. Sometimes he brings over groceries when we run low. Stuff they'd be throwing out anyway, he says, but I don't know, do you throw out cans of corn chowder and boxes of Froot Loops?"

No sound from Dad.

"Anyway, he's been pretty good. Helped me out at school, too. I was getting beat up every couple of days that first year. Buzzy heard about it, and one day he tells me he's going with me. I didn't want him to do it, but he walked right in the school yard and said, 'Point to 'em.'"

I heard Dad snoring softly. I sighed and got up to undress. In the bathroom I saw some clothes on the floor. They had black stains on them. When I picked them up, I smelled the boot polish. The trash basket was stuffed with paper towels, all smeared with polish.

I went and sat on the bed and looked out at the streetlight and wet pavement. The wind was knocking the bushes around, blowing up to a storm. I leaned my head against the window.

"Daddy," I whispered. "Daddy."

II

Dad sure has a way of stirring things up. We were all around the table, Dad, me, Donna, Betty, and this guy named Morty, who was just setting in a wheelchair smiling. He had on a Styrofoam helmet, and I saw he was tied into the chair with white straps.

Meanwhile, Donna was counting out the different pills like ammunition and putting them in little bottles, each with a label telling what each one was and when Dad had to take it.

Harry came in, pushing his IV stand. "What's going on?"

"We're going fishing," said Dad. "Cooter and me. Three days, right, Coot?"

"Right, Dad!"

"There's a place over by Strawn I always had luck at," he said.

"Now pay attention, John," said Donna. "You can

talk later. We got to get these pills straight. You got your money?"

"Right here." He showed her the small yellow envelope he had stuck in his shoe. "Two hundred dollars."

"Two hundred dollars! You rob a bank?"

Dad grinned. "Robbed my own bank."

"He's our rich resident," said Betty. "Disability, plus the pension."

"I'm going to be richer. Wait till I get my inventions going."

We were ready finally, and Nurse Betty took the van and drove us to the bus station. Boy, it was good to get away from the unit and breathe some air. Dad was in a state, though. He held on to me like he thought somebody was going to jump us. Betty carried our stuff and had the driver put it in the baggage hold. Then she straightened my cap on my head.

"You take care of your dad, now."

"I will, Betty."

"I know you will. You make sure he takes those pills."

"I will."

We climbed on aboard. "Wave, Dad," I said when the bus pulled out. Dad waved, and I saw Betty kind of laugh and shake her head.

Once we were on the highway he started to relax. Pretty soon he was telling the people on both sides how many fish we was going to catch in that stream he knew about. The way he is, looking straight at you, I don't think anybody even figured out he was blind. Crazy, maybe. He either annoys the life out of you or he makes you happy as you ever been.

Down in Strawn it was raining as bad as Kansas City. Dad told me about a motel we should get to and I got a taxi to take us. The room wasn't much bigger than Dad's room at the unit, except it had a kitchenette next to the hall closet. He tucked some money in my pocket and sent me around to the superette for sandwich stuff and Honey Nut Cheerios and a six-pack of Coors. When I got back, he had a country station on the radio, and he'd kicked his shoes off and was lying with his hands behind his head. He had me pop open a can for him.

"Pretty good life, huh, Cooter?"

"The best, Dad."

"You going to be ready tomorrow morning early?"

"Sure."

I went to the medicine box and set out his pills, like Donna told me. He gulped them down with the beer. After a while, I flipped on *Wheel of Fortune* and practiced shuffling with one hand while Dad smoked. Then we headed down to the restaurant.

Next morning, we had our spinning rods set to go, and baloney sandwiches wrapped up, and the old tackle box packed with flies and lures that Dad said always worked for him. The trouble was, the sun never came up. Night just got lighter, so I could see the rain sweeping across the parking lot.

"Rain don't last more than three days," he said, "and it's been that."

The taxi driver who took us was shaking his head when he let us out. We thought we'd be all right with our rain gear, but the wind blew under our ponchos, soaking our legs. Dad was holding on to me, and we almost went down together in the muddy field.

Finally we got to the water and found a place away from the trees so we could cast. I looked out over the stream, brown and swollen with flood. I couldn't imagine any fish would be interested in anything we would throw them, and it turned out I was right. Dad got his line snagged on an underwater branch and lost his best lure, a small silver spinner. Then he caught the back of his head with a cast.

After an hour of this we were both shaking, but I wasn't going to say anything. Finally he did.

"Well, son, do you think we caught enough for one morning?"

"I guess."

"Maybe we better leave a few for another day. Don't want to fish the place clean."

We scrambled up the bank and headed across the field to the road, two of the forlornest creatures you ever saw. I was hoping we'd get picked up, but maybe nobody wanted to get the inside of their car that wet. It took us an hour to walk it. Dad didn't stop shaking, so I got him to bed and fed him his pills. Then I started a cup of instant on the hot plate for him, but when I looked over, he was snoring. I sat there sipping the coffee and watching him.

For a joke, we both ordered fish for dinner, and he pretended they were ones we caught. Dad was getting back his old spirits. "What do you say we go bowling tonight?" he said, as we were rounding off the pecan pie.

"Great!"

"Ever been?"

"You took me. Remember?"

He didn't, but you couldn't blame him after five years and what else he's been through.

"You know I used to be semipro," he said, and I said I knew.

"Two-seventy-six," I said. "Right?" He was surprised I would've remembered the exact number of his best score. I was only nine years old the last time, so he had a lot to tell me. Maybe I could get as good as he was, but I would have to practice, practice.

All the way to the bowling alley he kept talking about the way to hold on to the ball and how to let it go. Then he told me about some of the great games he'd been in.

"How well do you think you'll do tonight, Dad?"

"Can't say. I never tried it without seeing."

"You'll do great, Dad."

"I still have some gas in me, don't I, son?"

Then he burst out singing, "I Don't Need Your Rocking Chair," real loud, right there in the taxi. I saw the driver looking at us in the rearview. Heck with him. I sang along at the top of my lungs.

"Woo hoo!" Dad yelled.

We burst into the bowling alley laughing like crazy, and they gave us a lane down at the end. I don't guess I'll ever forget that night. I laced Dad into his shoes and we went to pick out some balls. It had been a while, and everything felt real heavy to him, even the lightest ones with the smallest finger holes. Finally he took a pink one with sparkles. Good he couldn't see it.

I pointed him in the right direction and stepped back. He looked real good, with the perfect form he'd been teaching me about, letting the ball go just so. But I don't know how, that ball bounced hard and jumped the gutter and rolled down the lane next to us. They were real nice about it.

The next throw he didn't do it so hard, and it just rolled down the gutter, kind of quiet.

My turn wasn't so much better, though I kept it in our own gutter both times. Dad kept going. He thought he'd be able to hear where the pins were, but there was so much commotion all around us it was hard. One time he threw his ball the same time the guy next to us was throwing his. Dad's ball just clipped off one pin on the left side, but the other guy hit a strike, and everybody shouted, the girl especially. She was jumping up and down.

Daddy looked at me real excited.

"What'd I do, son? Tell me."

That's where I made a mistake. I didn't answer right away. I remembered what our minister said about lying and going to hell. By the time I spoke up, Dad's face had lost that great look.

"You did real well."

He brushed past me. "For a second there I thought I had something."

"No, really. I mean, it wasn't a strike exactly."

"How many?"

"How many? Four. Maybe five."

So I was going to hell anyway.

He shook his head. "Well," he said, "I guess that beats a gutter ball."

So we kept playing. I could see his neck getting red and I said maybe we should rest a minute, I'd get us some Cokes. He took the envelope out of his shoe and gave me a ten from it.

I didn't like leaving him alone, I don't know why. If anybody knows his way around a bowling alley it's my old man. I got the Cokes and two large popcorns and was starting back.

"Dad, no!" I yelled, but of course he didn't hear. He must've thought he was facing straight down the lane toward the pins, except he was facing the other way, toward the concession stand. He made a careful windup and then let go, just right.

"Dad!" I called, sloshing the Cokes as I ran. I saw a guy yank his girlfriend away.

"I don't hear the ball," said Dad.

"Of course you don't!"

"I don't hear the pins. What did I hit?"

"You hit a door."

"What? I hit a door? In a bowling lane?"

"You didn't *throw* it in the lane."

He started to say something, but stopped. I led him to the bench. "Here, Dad, drink this Coke. I better get the ball."

I had to apologize to a few people, but I got it. When I got back I found Dad with Coke spilled all down his black silk shirt. He had tears in his eyes.

"Dad, how'd you do that?"

"Cooter," he said, "get me out of here."

III

The worst part about coming back was everybody wanted to know about our great adventures. And the worst part about that is, Dad told them. Only he didn't tell it like I remembered it. He made everything funny. Even catching his own head with a fishhook, he had the nurses with tears in their eyes from laughing. And him bowling in the wrong direction and people running to get out of the way, that was the funniest thing you ever heard.

Back in the room with the door closed, he got real quiet. He was tireder than I ever seen him, and it seemed like the bones in his face was sticking out more.

I looked at him a long time.

"Daddy," I said.

"What, son?"

It was hard to say, so I said, "Could you turn the music down a minute?"

He cut the sound.

"Dad, do you think we could pray a little?"

He looked over at me. He didn't laugh or anything. "I don't know, son. I'm not much for that."

"That's okay."

"I guess we could try if you want."

"Well, no, I guess not."

"You know," he said, "I'm planning on licking this thing."

"I know it."

I guess he heard something in my voice, because he kind of reached over and hugged me to him.

Nurse Betty came in then. "I'll come back," she said.

Dad broke away. "That's okay. What is it, Sweetheart?"

"No, no."

"Come on, Bet," he said.

"Well, it's just that Rob—you won't believe this, but

Rob wants to know if anybody feels like playing a game of poker. I guess you inspired him."

Rob the skeleton. Rob the mute.

"We'll be right out," said Dad.

The funny thing was, Rob beat the pants off us. Eight dollars and twenty cents. Must've been that poker face of his. You couldn't tell what he was thinking. And I thought, *that's* the way to do it, just look like you're not even there.

I left the unit the next day. Dad promised to call me, and maybe when the weather got warm I could come up again. Then Betty started the van and I had to say good-bye. Dad tucked some tens in my shirt pocket.

"Don't you worry, son. I'll be fine."

"I know, Dad."

"Practice that shuffling. I want it real smooth next time I see you."

All the way back to Arkansas I watched out the window at the wet fields and dark little farm towns. I tried praying but couldn't get anywhere with it. All I could think of was how bony his chest was when he hugged me.

Dad called that same night. He sounded good. He called a couple times a week after that. Gradually I got back in my routine. I got a book out of the library about twenty ways to win at poker, and I practiced until I could beat Uncle Buzzy about three times out of five. Dad sounded pleased on the phone, although Mom wasn't, she wanted to take my cards away. Once she did, but I got more. They don't cost but a dollar.

I was getting pretty good, not just five-card stud, but draw and seven-card, too. I won enough to buy myself a little tape recorder. For my fifteenth birthday Dad made copies of his best albums and sent them down to me. I played that thing all the time.

Mom got me a bike for my birthday. It was a used one Uncle Buzzy had been working on, painting it red and putting on light blue streamers. Well, the streamers had to go. The way my school is, that would've been like wearing a sign, "Hit me."

Mom kept wanting me to go out and ride around more. Enjoy myself, she said, instead of staying in my room listening to tapes and working on my card games. She didn't understand if you want to get good at something you got to work at it.

Then around the middle of May I stopped hearing from Dad. I called the unit and Betty got on the phone. She said I better come right up. Mom didn't try to stop me. "You be safe, Cooter. Come straight home after you see him."

I had a seat to myself and set out a game of solitaire. I must've played twenty games, until finally the driver called out Kansas City. Betty was there to meet me, and she drove straight to the V.A. hospital. That's where they took Dad after he started bleeding inside.

We found out his room, 503, East Wing. Betty said she'd wait downstairs so I could be alone with him.

I went up, and finally somebody pointed out the right hallway. Room 503 was tiny, as crowded as a closet, and loud from some TV announcer shouting about what was behind curtain number one. The TV audience was laughing and clapping.

In all that confusion there was Dad lying on the bed,

naked as day. His eyes were mostly shut, but a little open, like he didn't have the energy to shut them all the way. His hair was all messed up, nobody combed it, and he needed a shave. Then I saw his wrists were tied with strips of cloth to the bed rails.

He didn't wake up and I didn't expect he would, if all that noise from the TV didn't wake him. What bothered me most was that they had him tied. I didn't like the tube in his nose, either, or the one in his arm.

I reached carefully and pulled up the sheet till it covered his middle.

"What are you *doing?*" The voice made me jump. It was a nurse coming in. She was young and in a hurry.

"Why do you have him tied down?"

"Are you related?"

"He's my dad."

She nodded, but kept moving things around, looking for something. "We had to restrain him," she said. "He started ripping the tubes out."

"He doesn't look like he's ripping any tubes out now."

"What?" She couldn't hear with that television.

"He's not ripping any tubes out *now.*"

"No, well now we have him on a morphine drip."

"What for?"

"Damn!" She picked up her clipboard. "I'm lost without this."

She went away and Dad and I were alone in this tiny room filled with screaming laughter. I reached up and slammed my fist on the button and the TV went off. You never saw a room get so quiet.

"Is that better, Dad?"

It was eerie him not saying anything. I reached over and untied his wrists, then I pulled back. His arm was cool. I rubbed it but it didn't get warmer.

"They shouldn't have done that, Daddy. I don't like that." I felt the tears starting and I wiped my eyes with my sleeve. I took a deep breath and I was able to stop. "Hey," I said, "I brought a pack of cards." I pulled off the rubber band. "Watch this."

I did the fancy one-hand shuffle I'd been practicing. The cards arched up in my palm like a bridge, then kind of shushed together.

"What do you think?"

Suddenly this nurse comes back carrying a basin. She looks at Dad, then she looks at him harder. She picks up his wrist and drops it.

"You'll have to leave," she says.

I just stood there.

"Did you hear me? Go on, we've got a dead man here."

I shook my head. "I'll go when I'm finished talking to my dad."

"You don't understand," she said.

I didn't move or look at her.

"Are you hard of hearing?" she said. "You can come back when I'm done."

"No," I said, real quiet. "You can come back when *I'm* done."

"What did you say?" She was holding that basin like she was going to hit me with it.

My voice stayed quiet. "I said get out."

She looked at me with her pretty blue eyes. "I'm going to have to call security."

Suddenly I screamed, *"Get out!"*

Her eyes kind of flattened. She didn't say a word, just edged past me. I held on to the bed rail till I stopped shaking.

"So what did you think? That was my right hand, but I can shuffle with my left, too. Oh, and take a gander at this." I set down my bag and took out the tape recorder.

"I got this from the money I made playing cards. A lot of kids won't play me anymore, did you know that?"

I pressed the button, and a guitar started, nice and slow. "Remember, Dad? Diamond Rio."

I felt a gentle hand on my back. It was Betty. She didn't say anything, just put her arm around my waist and stood next to me a long time.

Out in the parking lot, the trees were all white. It was a hot day and the air was heavy with the stink of pear blossoms and car exhaust. Betty got out her keys. I closed my eyes and took a breath, deep as I could, like I wanted to remember that smell forever.

A Note From the Author

I'm not sure why I started volunteering at an AIDS facility back in 1992. Anger, probably. I was mad that thousands of Americans were shunned and discriminated against because they happened to have a deadly illness. I quickly learned not to use the term "AIDS victim," because the people I got to know did not behave like victims. The father in my story "What Are You Good At?" is based on a guy I knew at the nursing facility. The fact that he was blind and dying was clearly less important to him than teaching his kid how to fish. Near the end, I promised I'd write a story for him. He was in a coma, and I don't know if he ever heard me, but I finally kept my promise. I'm glad I did.

ATOMIC BLUE PIECES

ANGELA JOHNSON

Somebody told me once you can't die from pain, even if you want to.

You can make your world what you want it to be sometimes.

So there wasn't any pain for me, for a while.

While I was lying there all I could think about was how I was supposed to take out the garbage at home. No pain. I had a dental appointment on Friday—Mama would have to write me an excuse to get out of school. No pain. And I was never letting my best friend, Cougar, use my notes from American history again. He must have lived his whole life on pizza, and my notes proved it.

No pain. No busted leg. No pain.

If you count between thunderclaps during a storm you'll know whether the storm is coming or going during the next count. Lower number—it's coming at you. Higher number—it's leaving.

I can count during a storm.

• • •

The day my brother Leon left I broke my leg falling down the steps of an old deserted building that Mama had told me not to go in. I lay there half a day.

I remember Cougar picking me up and running down the broken steps two at a time. I remember how it hurt so much just before we got out of the place I saw a flash of white light and passed out.

No more pain.

The morning before Leon left he shared half his toast with me and most of his bacon. We didn't get bacon that much, either. He'd sat there smiling at me while I picked out of his plate and babbled about nothing.

Mama had already told me to shut up, twice. Leon had shot her dirty looks, though, and smiled back at me.

I'd eaten one more piece of Leon's bacon and had run my bare feet underneath the chair. The linoleum was gritty and cold. Leon kept on smiling.

When I found out that night after I'd gotten back from the emergency room that Leon was gone I stared out the kitchen window until Mama yelled at me that I was just like that "damned Leon." When she stomped out the room I took an Atomic Blue Magic Marker and wrote my brother's name all over my cast.

The day my brother Leon left was mostly white light and pain. But it also was atomic blue, bacon, and his face. Atomic Blue and Leon's smiling face all around.

Chalky's Trailer Park is wedged up against Route 82 and Cave Man Woods. So everybody who grows up there spends most of their lives listening to grown people yelling at them to stay off the highway and not to go into the swamp woods.

That meant until you are sixteen or have a friend who can drive you're stuck at Chalky's. My days stuck around here were coming to an end. I'd steal a car and drive to hell if I had to, 'cause even though I'd been stuck, I'd had Leon and Cougar. We'd all hung out in the swamp like all the kids who lived at Chalky's.

It was all something else then. Something I could live with.

I'd walked down Route 82 with anybody who was sure their parents weren't going to be coming down the road and waving us back to Chalky's.

Didn't they know that they couldn't keep us locked up and away from everything that we were looking for? Didn't they know that sooner or later . . .

Sooner or later . . .

Maybe Mama knew about sooner or later. Maybe she knew it as she stood processing turkeys at Bil-Mars.

Maybe she knew it when she'd go out with her girlfriends and drink beers at Star Lanes Bowling while smiling at men who worked at Bil-Mars and were out with their friends.

Maybe she even knew about sooner or later when she'd sit in the front window of our trailer all night long listening to Sam Cooke records and playing solitaire. Sometimes getting me up to drink a cup of hot chocolate with her in winter and lemon iced tea in the summer, always at 3:00 A.M. She called this time the hour of souls and she didn't want to be alone when the clock chimed to three.

I only remember Mama at these times because of extremes. Extreme cold. Extreme heat.

Leon says Mama is intense. And I wondered out loud once if that was the reason our dad left. Leon got mad when he heard me say it. He turned away from me and whispered, "She got intense after he left us."

If I'd known Leon would leave us for good I would have paid him back the ten dollars I owed him for fronting me movie tickets and nachos last month. For the last few days it's all I can think about. I figure he could probably use that ten. He could buy a lot of nachos with it.

He could buy bottled water. He drank it all the time.

I still dream that he'll come back for the money. Ten dollars is a lot of money when you have nothing. Did he have anything? Was he warm and safe?

Did he think about us?"

Me and Mama walking around like ghosts at Chalky's. Mama wanting to stay home and go looking for him but knowing she couldn't afford to lose her job. Me waking up in the middle of history class calling out his name.

Was he thinking about us?

In the end Leon had to go because no one but me would believe him. And that was funny 'cause Leon is the most honest person in the world. So honest that sometimes I didn't think he belonged in this century.

Leon talked about honor and loyalty. Not the stupid kind where people don't tell when they see their friends hurt or kill somebody.

Leon has honor and morality that Mama always used to

be proud of until it brought the cops and social services to our trailer.

Honor and loyalty is just fine I guess as long as it doesn't visit you when you least expect it and get in the way of your life.

Was Leon thinking about us?

He'd play the African drums on the top of Selby's drugstore, well, what used to be Selby's. Leon said he loved to watch everybody from above—six stories above. He wanted to play the drums for everybody.

He did.

Sweet, faraway drumming all over the town.

Leon would drum on top of Selby's in the morning and just as the sun was going down. He'd drum everybody in Springhill awake and asleep. Sweet, faraway drumming like he was calling to people he never met in a country he'd never been to.

Leon's drumming made me sad. 'Cause I knew. I knew what I didn't want to know. Leon was not one of us. Even the us everybody our age in Springhill would probably become whether we wanted to or not.

He wouldn't work at the turkey farm or go to Star Lanes on Friday night. He wouldn't stand along the fence watching high school football and talking about how he could have been.

He'd never put on a pig roast and stand around a bonfire passing a paper bag full of whiskey that stung you all the way down, like a lot did years after they couldn't run fast anymore and the weather channel was more important to them than the world news.

I know if Leon had stayed in the county and went to football games, the boy who drummed for us would be gone forever.

The boy who used to let me sit beside him and draw while he drummed would just vanish in the mist like people did in scary books. The boy who let me draw him drumming in blue as the sun set would disappear. And he did.

Mama cries all the time now, but I don't really think she's crying for Leon. I think she's crying for all the ones who have left her. Not for their sake, but her own.

She keeps saying, "Just like his damned daddy."

And I'm just like that "damned Leon."

Daddy, Leon, and me are all damned in Mama's eyes. A whole trailer full of the damned.

Leon used to go to day camp with T-Boy James. They learned to swim together. But T-Boy had stuff happen to him. He changed from the kid who used to share his pudding with my brother. He turned nasty and dangerous. His grandma cried when they dragged him away.

When T-Boy James got out of juvenile it didn't take him long to start messing with everybody that he thought put him there. That was a lot of people 'cause T-Boy did everything but kill before they finally locked him up. He'd spent two years in Holcomb and some people say he'd had a bad time there 'cause there is always somebody badder in the world.

Cougar got on the bus twice in two weeks with a bloody nose.

Somebody had broken every window out of the science lab and keyed all the police cars parked by the courthouse. There was other stuff, but the night the block of apartments across from Selby's went up in flames was one of the worst nights of my life.

An old lady didn't make it out.

And a couple of hours later men were looking under our trailer and knocking the door in and dragging Leon off.

Mama went and picked Leon up from the police station that night. Both her and the legal aid lawyer she brought with her looked overworked and nervous.

Leon came home sleepy and quiet. He hugged me hard just before he crawled into bed with all his clothes on. I didn't know it then, but I only had a week to be in the company of my brother.

I used to wonder what would happen to me when Leon went away. I used to think that I'd probably miss him so bad, it would hurt. But I thought away meant college or a job in another state, so he'd come back to me and my loneliness . . .

I do not know the woman who calls herself my mother. She doesn't really know me.

Leon knows both of us, though.

But now he's gone.

In the end it didn't matter that T-Boy heard Leon drumming on Selby's roof when he poured the first drops of gasoline or that he hid the gas can under our trailer. It doesn't even matter that everybody would have found out the truth about Leon in the end.

It's about pain.

T-Boy's pain, Leon's pain, everybody's pain. The pains might never even have had to come together for my brother to leave this town. But he did. He did in broad daylight with a backpack and his drum under one arm. A man getting to the turkey farm late for work saw him get in a semi off Route 44.

He said he was smiling when he got in.

I can't believe that though, 'cause I heard Leon on the roof way after that man says he got in the truck. I can still smell the smoke of the gutted building across the street as I climbed the steps to the roof.

Sweet drumming.

Sweet Leon playing . . .

I even thought I heard him as I fell and visions of atomic blue drawings and pain shot through me.

I always count during the pain, now.

Two thousand one, two thousand two . . .

Higher numbers it's coming—lower numbers it's going away. My leg has healed and they knocked Selby's to the ground so no more accidents would happen there and no more boys who thought about somewhere else would sit on its roof.

Somebody told me once that you can't die from pain, but I don't remember who.

A Note From the Author

The very act of aging sets human beings up for loss.
There are a lucky few of us who manage to get through our
childhoods without any significant losses. Our grandparents
and closest relatives stay with us. Some people even keep
their pets until they leave home.

Of course, not everyone is as lucky. Some individuals are
born to loss. The characters in "Atomic Blue Pieces" seem
to realize their losses at a very early age. The mother, having
lost her happiness a long time ago, is distant and angry. The
brother and sister have lost a parent who could understand
them. Their closeness comes from knowing that truly
each is the only one the other has. And then a lie destroys any
hope the two siblings have of ever stopping all the ongoing
sadness that permeates their lives.

"Atomic Blue Pieces" tells a story of the kind of loss
that runs deepest: the loss of a loved one.

THE TIN BUTTERFLY

NORMA FOX MAZER

I
Mim and Her Sisters

You were born different," Mim's mother would say, giving her hoarse, cigarette-deepened laugh. "From the gitgo, you were my weird one. Like a duck with tadpoles or something. You know what I mean, honey, you were just different."

Mim, the duck, didn't have to ask different how. Quack, quack. You only had to look at the pictures in the baby albums. There were her sisters, all of them fat and smiling, all of them adorable and placid, the way babies were supposed to be. And there was Mim, not a smile in sight, not a hair on her head, staring out from her pinch of a face, as if she were already planning the questions she was going to torment her mother with as soon as she could talk. "Why are trees tall? Why is the sky up there and not down here? If you weren't my mother, who would you be? Where did yesterday go?"

"Lucky for me, you shut up after a while," her mother said.

Mim didn't know how to be like her sisters, how to be fat and sweet, how to tease, how to talk. They didn't really mind her silence, just sometimes. "What are you staring at now? Look at her. Look at Mim! She's figuring if she approves of the lot of us."

Oh, she did approve! She wanted to be like them, easy in the world, and it was hopeless. She was different, starting with her cutoff bit of a name. You could just mumble it out of your mouth. Hardly move your lips and it was gone. But their names! Her mother was Blossom, her father, Huddle Herbert, her sisters were Beauty, Faithful, Fancy, Autumn, Clarity, and Charity. Those were *names*. Outstanding. Uncommon. Ravishing.

Even Fancy, with her slow smile and slow brain, knew her name was special. "I'm real proud of my name," she'd say. "I'm *Fancy*." Autumn liked to point out that she had autumn-colored freckles splashed across her nose. "Parents named me sooo right," she would chortle. Beauty didn't have to say a word. She was the oldest girl and, true enough, beautiful.

Mim came after Beauty in order of age, but not in order of anything else. After Mim came Faithful. Her and her temper. Shorten her name to Faith—go on, just try it—-and her blue eyes would pop as if they were going to burst out of her face, and she'd shriek into *your* face, "*Dooon't* call me Faith. My name is *Faithful*."

Mim's mother had said she was through with babies

after Autumn, but six years later, along came the twins, Clarity and Charity. They were preemies and only lived a few months. Whenever the family visited the twins' graves, they brought candy and chips to picnic on. They'd sit around on a blanket, and Mim's mother would cry a little and talk about the babies and Mim would make up funny names for them: cutie pies, wonder eyes, belly button baby wonders, and anything else she could dream up.

As for her own name, she was used to it. Sometimes, she even quite liked it. "I quite like it," she said to herself. She would never say anything like that in front of her family. *Quite like?* Oh, no. But she did *quite like* saying those words. And she did *quite like* saying her name. Saying it under her breath, quick and low, running the sound into a single syllable, a long hum. And then, sometimes, this thing happened, which Mim called the Flash Feeling, when she got inside the sound, as if it had shape, as if it were a place. Maybe it was. A place called Not Here. In Not Here, she was a Mim who said things like *quite like* and *ravishing*. A Mim who talked and made jokes. A Mim like herself, but like them, too, her family: talkers, teasers, laughers, all pretty, all fat with round, soft arms and sweet rolls of fat around their bellies.

Only Mim, no matter how much she ate, stayed all knee knobs and elbow bumps. "Look at those legs," her sisters teased. "They are so pitiful. Where'd you get those toothpicks, honey, down at Brenda's Diner?"

Mim's father had been thin once, but he was fat now, too, although not in the round-and-soft-everywhere way that her mother and sisters were. "Muscle," he said, slapping his belly, "a hundred percent muscle." He told his daughters to hit him. "Right in the solar plexus. See for your silly selves. Muscle, all muscle."

They descended on him. "We'll get you, Daddy," Beauty cried. He kept them off, hands out, feinting one way, then the other. "Packa wild girls," he said, grinning his jack-o'-lantern smile.

Mim was there with her sisters, advancing on her father with fists bouncing, laughing and shrieking and then, suddenly, she noticed his mouth, the missing teeth, the empty spaces, and she stopped.

She knew he had missing teeth—of course, she did, but now it was like fresh bad news. His face, his poor face. His nose twisted from a fight he'd had as a boy, his mouth with those clownish gaps. It hurt her, hurt so much, she had to sit down.

"Come on, Mim!" her sisters cried.

"I'm not here," she gasped from the couch, scrunching her knees up to her chin. What did she mean by that? She had no idea. Her sisters hooted. "Oh, Mim! You are so weird."

II
City Ladies

City ladies, Mim's mother called the two women who had bought the old Patterson mansion on Fordych Hill. "City ladies are going to take a fall," she said, blowing smoke out of her nose. "Bed-and-Breakfast place here, in Mallory? Who's going to come, the moose?"

Mallory was close to the Canadian border, a town of

small hills that tapered off into the forest. Once, the town had been prosperous. Every day, on the way to school, Mim passed reminders of that time: the Victorian mansions with their towers and stained glass windows, the limestone Gothic church, the boarded-up opera house at the traffic corner. World famous singers had once appeared on that stage. Once there had been a busy hotel on Main Street, too, with, it was said, gold faucets in every sink. Men in three piece suits, who smoked expensive cigars, met there to talk business. Bootleg liquor was what had made Mallory rich. Booze. Hooch whiskey, brewed in stills hidden deep in the forest. Mim's great-grandfather had been one of those whiskey woodsmen, but if he'd gotten rich, they didn't know anything about it.

They weren't exactly poor, but whenever her father finished a job, he'd throw the money down on the kitchen table and say to Mim's mother, "Blossom darling, we eat this week."

Everyone in Mallory was the same, Mim's father said. "Doing their damn best to make a buck and put bread on the table." A lot of people worked at the state prison, fifteen miles out of town. The only place Mim's father would never take a job was at the prison. He was the Fixit Man. The hand-lettered sign on the side of his truck advertised, I FIX ANYTHING, ANYWHERE.

To help out, Mim's mother played the Lottery every Tuesday. Sometimes, she hit for five or ten dollars. Once, four hundred dollars. She'd gone right out and bought them all new clothes. It was time for the luck to hit again, she said, but meanwhile it was up to Mim's father. Lately, he'd been working for the city ladies.

Mim met them for the first time on a Saturday morning in October. She had come on an errand for her father. The city ladies were washing windows on the long porch. The tall one was standing on a chair to get to the top of the high windows. What Mim thought in those first moments was what anyone might think: that she had never seen a woman so tall and so thin. Like a giraffe, Mim thought. And about the other one, nothing at all, except that from the back she had shoulders like a man.

There was a pot of scarlet mums on the steps and several green wicker rockers on the porch. The tall one stepped off the chair. "Hello!" she said.

Mim saw a slash of red lipstick, a mass of gold wire hair, slightly bulging eyes. Those eyes seemed to look at Mim in a way no one ever had before. She's *seeing* me, Mim thought, and it scared her, as if the woman knew everything about her, all her secret thoughts.

III
Saturday Morning Pancakes

At breakfast that morning, Mim's father had said, "Those ladies over on Fordych Hill, they owe me money."

Mim's mother was at the stove, making pancakes. "How much do they owe you, HH?"

"A good chunk. I was up on that roof all week." He cut his stack of pancakes into quarters and the quarters into more quarters. He was a careful eater, as he was careful in his work. "They got more work than they're ever going to get done. Those ladies are working like fools trying to fix it up."

"That's the old Patterson place," Mim's mother said.

"Remember when the newspaper wrote a big article about him, Blossom darling? Old Baking Powder Prince built that place as a summer cottage for his wife." Mim's father looked around at his daughters. "Just a little cottage with twenty-five rooms and ten bathrooms. They needed one room just for their money," Mim's father said, cutting and chewing steadily.

Mim's mother flipped a pancake. "You better go on over there today and collect what's owed you."

"Oh, Mommy," Faithful and Beauty said, almost at the same time. "It's Saturday!"

"You see, your daughters know," Mim's father said. "They know I don't do nothing today. Nothing today and nothing tomorrow."

"These are my damn days off," Mim said, under her breath.

"These are my damn days off," her father said.

Mim's mother picked up her cigarette and took a puff. Then, slapping her spatula on the side of the pan, she said, "Only me, only me, I don't have no damn days off."

Mim's father almost leaped out of his seat. "Well, that's true, and I am sorry about it," he said, "but here's the rule. Who brings in the money gets to rest." He paused to let that sink in. "Like God. He worked hard all week and then He took His day off, and I ain't comparing myself, I'm just making a point."

For once, Mim's sisters were as silent as she, waiting to see how this conversation would finish. They'd heard it before, and almost always it ended with their mother saying something like, "You're right, HH. You are right! What would we do without you? Just go hungry!"

Sometimes, though, as she did this time, Blossom darling surprised them all. She left the stove, she left the pancakes in the pan, and she plunked herself down in a chair, big arms crossed, one hand holding her cigarette up in the air.

Everyone waited. Finally, Mim's father said, "Them pancakes are going to burn. Pancake maker gone on strike?"

Blossom just sat there, staring hard at her cigarette, as if it could tell her something she needed to know.

"Blossom," Mim's father said.

Still no response, just that hard, frowning stare upward. Just the cigarette snagged in her upraised hand. Just the unnatural silence.

"Blossom, what in hell are you thinking about so hard?"

"That damn ceiling is falling down," she said finally. "It's hanging all over us in pieces. You ever going to do anything about it, Mr. Fixit?"

"I'll fix it."

"Yeah, one of these days," she said. "One of these days when you get off of someone else's roof."

Then, silence again.

Finally, when they were all eyeing each other as if they couldn't bear it another moment, Mim's mother snuffed out her cigarette on the edge of a plate. "Who wants more pancakes?"

"We all do, you're the greatest cook, Blossom darling," Mim's father said.

Blossom snorted and wriggled her behind. "No money, but we're happy," she said, "Am I right or am I right?"

"You're right, Mommy," Mim and her sisters chorused raggedly, looking at their father and smiling. Everything was okay again.

Later, Mim's father sent her over to Fordych Hill to collect the money he was owed from the city ladies. "I can trust you not to stop and gab," he said. "Not like your sisters. You'll come right home."

IV
Wings

"Who are you?" the city lady with the broad shoulders said.

Mim stopped on the middle step. "Mim," she said. "Taylor," she added after a moment.

"What do you want?"

"Ell, stop that, you'll scare her." This was the tall one. She had green fingernails and wore a matching green chiffon scarf around her neck. "What can we do for you, Mim Taylor? Did you come to sell us Girl Scout Cookies?"

"Now, you're teasing her, Ruth." Ell went back to washing windows, turning her broad back to them.

"I wasn't teasing, but you wouldn't care, anyway, would you, Mim Taylor?"

Mim stood straight, hands in her back pockets. "No, I wouldn't," she said, wondering how the woman knew that about her. "My father sent me." Then it was the awkward business of getting out that she'd come to collect money owed him.

"Oh, Mr. Huddle Herbert is your dad. The Fixit Man. Ell, we didn't pay him. Shame on us!" Ruth put her hands to her face, but Mim could see that she wasn't ashamed at all. "I'll write you a check," she said. But before the check was produced, Mim must sit down, Mim must have a drink of fruit juice, Mim must have some cookies. She was hungry, wasn't she? Girls were always hungry.

"No, thank you," Mim said, sitting on the edge of one of the green rocking chairs.

"She's being polite," Ell advised, without looking around.

"Of course she is," Ruth said, "Mim Taylor, wait until you taste these cookies. I made them myself." She went into the house.

Ell continued washing windows. All along the street, the maples had turned brilliant red. Mim stood up. She thought of leaving, but she couldn't, not without the money.

Ruth came back with a tray holding cookies, juice, and the check for Mim's father. "Sit down, Mim." She put the tray on a table and called Ell. "Stop working, and come and talk to this child."

Child? Mim didn't consider herself a child. "I'm thirteen," she said.

"Oh, really! I should have known you were older than you look," Ruth said. "Now, can you tell what Ell is, besides a super window washer?"

Mim shifted on her chair and regarded Ell. "I think she's . . . an artist," she guessed.

"All right, that's good! She's a musician, a pianist. She once played in Carnegie Hall. Do you know what Carnegie Hall is, Mim Taylor? No?" And then the intense gaze. "It's in New York City, where you have to go someday."

"All right," Mim said, to be polite.

"Ah! If you do it, then you'll help redeem my life."

"Stop that, Ruth," Ell said. "Your life doesn't need redeeming."

"No, it does! I'm been mostly a useless human being, Mim, taken care of by others, but not any more. But now, Mim, I make it possible for Ell to go on with her music. You can't deny that, can you, Ell?"

"I won't deny it," Ell said, taking a cookie from the plate.

"I'll tell everyone, Mim," Ruth surged on, "and I'll tell you, we're making a home for ourselves and at the same time welcoming guests into it, who will help us go on living here."

Mim nodded. It seemed a fine arrangement to her.

"And Ell gets to practice the piano four, five, even six hours a day. When we have guests, she plays for them, and I believe that one of these days, someone will be here who knows music, and they'll hear her—"

Ell had gone back to washing the window. "You're getting too excited, Ruth. Stop," she said.

Ruth nibbled a cookie. "Ell is right, as always. She's not only a great musician, she's full of common sense. Do you like school, Mim? Tell me about it. Tell me about yourself. Don't let me dominate the conversation!"

At home, no one cared if she was silent. That was Mim, they were used to her. But Ruth leaned forward. She wanted to hear what Mim had to say, insisted on hearing it. But what was there to say? School? It was just something she did every day. "I like parts of school," she said, stupidly.

"All right. Parts of it. Let's try something else. What will you do when you're through with school?"

"I don't know."

"College?"

Mim shook her head.

"And why not?"

"No money."

"Ahh. Money! Don't forget this." She handed Mim the check for her father. "Now . . . what would you do, if money wasn't a problem?"

"I don't know."

"Oh, you do. I know you do."

Mim stared at Ruth. "I like to draw clothes," she said. One of her secrets. "I make creations. Different things."

"Splendid! Do you know there's a fashion institute in New York? Now we know why you must go there."

Mim nodded, knowing she would go nowhere. She would stay in Mallory, just as her sisters would. "Has anyone ever put wings on an evening dress?" Immediately, she regretted saying it. It was too strange. She had never let anyone see those drawings.

"That really is a delightful idea," Ruth said, "but I see some practical problems. You'd have to make them very light, wouldn't you? What kind of material would you use? Would they flutter like butterfly wings, or be kind of stiff like a dragonfly? Would they fold when you put on a jacket?"

When Mim left Ruth and Ell, her father's check safely in her pocket, she was late. She ran all the way home. She flew as if she had wings. Her feet never touched ground.

V

The House on Fordych Hill

Through the winter, once or twice a week after school, Mim walked up Fordych Hill and stopped in to see Ruth and Ell. They were always busy, Ruth working on the house, scrubbing or painting, wearing jeans and an old shirt. She was never without a pale chiffon scarf floating around her neck.

"Oh, good!" Ruth would say. "Ell, here's Mim come to keep us company."

Ell was either working with Ruth or practicing the piano. Ell, Mim thought, was something like a grown-up *her*: she didn't say much, you could never tell what she was thinking. Mim liked to sit in a corner of the front room and listen to her playing, watching her hands over the keys, and the way her broad back swayed one way, then the other. Even away from the piano, her hands were always slightly in motion. If air was water, Mim thought, then Ell's hands were the faintest ripples of wind over that water.

Mim talked to Ruth, listened to Ell play the piano. She stayed half an hour, an hour, never longer. And when she left, closing the heavy front door with its leaded windows carefully behind her, it was as if she stepped out of a world she could only have imagined.

63

Walking home through the snow, she went over her conversation with Ruth, word by word. And behind the words, she heard the music again, coloring everything.

One day Ruth talked about dreams and love. "Love is the most important thing, Mim, and dreams are part of love. Dreams can come true. Oh, that sounds so corny! But I truly believe it. You have to keep trying for what you want and what you love in life. And you should never stop dreaming."

"I know that," Mim said, but the truth was that she didn't really understand it all then. It wasn't the words— the words were easy. To know fully what Ruth meant, though, to know for herself, in her skin and in her bones that what Ruth had said was true, would take years.

Mim's mother said, "Are you making a nuisance of yourself to those city ladies? What do you want with them, anyway? You're just a kid."

Mim hunched her shoulders. "They're . . ." She searched for the right word. ". . . fascinating."

"Fascinating! Listen to that! Leave it to you to say something like that." Her mother knuckled Mim's head. "You just got your own little drummer up there, don't you? But watch out, don't be like me. Don't overdo things." Her mother's voice rang in Mim's ears. "You see me with the cigarettes? I love my ciggies, but I overdo them. You hear my voice?" She coughed. "That's from overdoing. Once you start overdoing, you can't stop yourself."

Mim knew she overdid things. She overdid her imagination. She overdid being quiet. She overdid her concentration when she worked on her drawings. She tried not to overdo her welcome with Ell and Ruth. She tried to stay away more. What if, one day, they looked at her, pointed their fingers—Ell's so fine and long, Ruth's so white and soft—and said, "You've overdone it! Out. And don't come back."

VI
Clown Turned Downside Up

Guests were coming to Ruth and Ell's B&B, but never many, no more than three or four in a week. And some weeks that winter, none at all. Then, Ell was gloomy. "Why would anyone come here, anyway?" she said. "Trek all the way up here? What for? This is the armpit of the state."

"Nooo," Ruth cried. "It's so beautiful here." She began listing reasons why people would come to Mallory. To see the leaves in fall, to walk the mountain trails in winter, to smell the flowers in spring, and what about the good, clean air. "And-and-and to hear the water running down the mountains!" she said. "Yes, Ell? Yes? And remember, some people are going to have business with the hospital, and maybe the state prison."

Ell shuddered. "Don't even mention it."

"We knew it would be slow in the beginning," Ruth said. "We'll get more people. Have faith, darling. Word of mouth, remember? And meanwhile, we're living and working in our own place, and we're happy. Aren't we happy?"

Ell merely raised her eyebrows.

Mim mused on that word, *happy*, on the way home. What, exactly, was it? How did you know if you were happy? She was pretty sure she wasn't, but she wasn't unhappy, either. She thought she was somewhere in between, suspended between the two, like the wooden clown doll her father had brought home once. When you squeezed the sticks attached to the clown's hands, he turned head over heels, upside down and downside up. Release the stick, and he just hung there with his fixed clown smile.

One day when Mim stopped by the house on Fordych Hill, Ruth and Ell were in a rush of work. "Eight people are coming," Ruth said, her cheeks feverish. "Eight in one party! They called late this afternoon. They'll be here in an hour."

"We'll get everything done, stop worrying," Ell said. She was carrying a pile of linen up the stairs.

"I'll help," Mim said. She took the linen from Ell. She knew the drill. She had watched them prepare for guests.

After that day, she always joined in when there was work to do. She made beds and hung fresh towels in the bathrooms. Ruth wanted to pay her, but Mim refused. "I like to help you," Mim said. "I'll always help you."

"You been there again?" her mother said.

Mim nodded.

"Helping them, I suppose?"

"Yes."

"Hon, if you worked just as hard earning money at a real job . . . wouldn't you like that? You could be like your dad, come home, put your pay on the table, keep something for yourself, and help out your family at the same time."

"I'm sorry," Mim said.

But even though she didn't earn money, she did keep something for herself. She kept her happiness for herself. She kept every moment she was with them for herself.

One afternoon, Ruth and Mim were cleaning the high cupboards in an upstairs bedroom that had once been a maid's room. It connected to the kitchen by a back stairway. It was a mess. The house was silent. Ell had gone out for a walk. "She gets restless," Ruth said. "She misses the city."

They talked as they worked, Mim not saying a lot, but always aware how Ruth spoke to her, as if she were someone. A real person. Without knowing how it happened, she found herself telling Ruth about the Flash Feeling, how sometimes it came when she was bent over her homework at the kitchen table, elbowed in by her sisters. How she'd be inside the words, in the sound.

"It's a feeling like flying. I don't mean airplanes, I've never even been on one. I mean what flying would be like if you could just lift your arms and *go*. Soar. Sometimes, though, it's like a color, like swimming in a color."

She'd said too much. She sounded crazy.

"You're different, aren't you?" Ruth said.

Different. That word that had clanged through her life. Mim scrubbed at the shelf. If she had a gallon of paint, she'd throw it in here, wipe out the old spots, the old dirt, every little smudge that showed.

"You're not just another kid. You pretend, but you're different," Ruth said, and then more, a long, rushed blur of words.

"Mim," Ruth said. "Look at me."

Mim turned, planning her escape. Down the ladder, the stairs, out the door, never come back. She had told all, revealed all. She was skinned and half-dead. She put a smile on her face, a stiff, wooden smile.

"Mim." Ruth's slightly bulging eyes were fixed on her, holding her there.

Mim stared at Ruth's hair, half-hidden under a kerchief. It matched the raspberry colored scarf around her neck. "Why do you wear those scarves all the time? Is something wrong with your throat?"

Ruth touched the scarf. "Nothing now. I have a scar."

"Why?" Mim demanded.

Ruth shook her head. "It's all in the past. I don't like to talk about it. There's joy now, every day, why think of old bad things? Child, did you hear what I said before?"

"What?" Gradually, though, Ruth's words came back, as if in separate little parcels, which rearranged themselves into sentences. "Different isn't bad, don't look so stricken. Don't you know you're a delightful person?"

Mim's stomach chilled. Was it true? What exactly had Ruth said? *Different isn't bad.* She went over it in her mind. She tried to believe it.

VII
The Tin Butterfly

It was spring. A weak sun melted the snow into puddles. Mim walked into the house without knocking. She moved quietly across the patterned rug. In the front room, she saw Ruth and Ell sitting across from each other in the matching wing chairs. Their knees touched, they were holding hands.

"Darling," Ruth was saying, "it will be all right."

Ell nodded, laid her head against Ruth's knees.

"Baby," Ruth said.

Mim made a sound, and Ruth turned. Ell rose immediately and went to the piano. She ran her hands over the keys. Birds rose from under her fingers . . . water, wind.

Ruth smiled absently. She was watching Ell.

Mim shivered, lonely, as if she wasn't even with them.

Ruth and Ell left Mallory in June. They had used all their savings, gone into debt. Ell had a summer job playing the piano at a resort hotel. Ruth would work nearby as a hostess in a restaurant. In the fall, well, in the fall they'd figure out something else.

The day they left, Mim was there to say goodbye. Ell was in the passenger seat, Ruth behind the wheel of their car. She wore sunglasses and bright red lipstick, and the raspberry scarf floated around her neck. She took off her sunglasses. "Mim," she said, "think well of yourself."

Mim held her hands across her stomach. She was incapable of saying anything. Her grief was too large for words.

"And leave," Ruth said. "When the time comes, go. Try things."

Mim nodded. She would leave, but it was distant. A long time in the future. Years away. She could hardly envision it, but she knew she would go. And just for a moment she understood it all—how loss came to everyone. How it was part of life, like the leaves coming off the trees in autumn and the snow melting in spring. How she would lose her place in her family. How she would leave them, and they would let her go. And how she would never see Ruth and Ell again.

Ruth turned the key in the dashboard. "Goodbye, Mim." The engine coughed. "Remember us."

"Wait," Ell said. She fumbled in a canvas bag and then leaned across Ruth to hand Mim a tiny, pressed tin butterfly. "We want you to have this."

It was cool, almost weightless in her hand, perched on its tiny legs, as if it were about to rise. "It's really for me?" She had never owned anything so beautiful.

She lunged to kiss Ell's hand, her lips landing with a smack. Tears shot to her eyes at her clumsiness in this moment, when everything should have been grace and perfection.

And then it was finished. They were gone. She stood there, in front of the darkened house, watching the white car glide down the street, between the trees. The sun had gone down. The light was fading, but the sky was still brightly lit.

From the Author

*This is a story that I have wanted to write ever since
I met two splendid and unique women in an Adirondack
camp for adults, where I was working at the age of sixteen,
as possibly the worst waitress they ever hired. These women,
either out of sheer generosity of spirit or some kind of
second sight, befriended me, a shy and awkward teenage
girl, and, when they left, gave me a small, enameled
butterfly pin. Somewhere along the line, I lost the pin,
but I never forgot it, or the women. Still, it was only while
writing this story that I came to understand what they had
done for me those many years ago, how they had given
me another, more subtle gift: an opinion of myself as more
than I was then, an opinion that leaped years ahead to
whom I might become.*

THE FIRE POND

MICHAEL J. ROSEN

We stock the fire pond with rainbows. "Fire pond's" a thing I've said for fourteen years and never once thinking what it means besides this lake that Grandpa and friends dug behind the barn before I was born— before Dad was born. It's perfect for swimming, if you're not afraid of snakes (which you shouldn't be since snakes are more scared of you), and it's clear, so you can see your legs treading water underneath. The pond's large enough to row around in a boat, and good for skating, too, unless you're hotdogging and trying those Olympic-medal spins. It's a place the cows and horses will drink—deer, too, though we'd rather they hang out at another farm and leave our crops alone.

The rainbows are Grandpa's. A few times a summer, we fish out half a dozen for supper. Sometimes we'll catch them on these hooks that don't have barbs, so we can measure the trout and release them again. But the rainbows aren't really for eating, just like the pond's not really for raising fish.

On the ride back from school, I stop and pick up loaves of two-day-old bread that Angela at the bakery holds for Grandpa (her mom was Grandpa's girlfriend before he met Grandma) and, every now and then, a piece of lung the butcher saves. Then Grandpa chops it all up and showers handfuls around the dock so the rainbows surface, blurring Grandpa's reflection until it's gone and, looking down, the fish are all you can see.

He talks to the fish whether I'm there or not. Tells them stuff the way I guess I talk to the cats when they follow me around the barn.

"I do all the talking," Grandpa says. "I'm not expecting them to answer."

We have two farm cats—and also this Lab–shepherd mix that's owned by Mrs. Collins, except he spends all day across the road at our place following whoever of us is on the tractor. Grandpa never takes much notice of them. The rainbows are what he's got instead of pets—instead of lots of things. He walks the edge of the fire pond every day, just looking, just admiring what he's got there. It's like the story about the king—or was it the thief?—who has to count his riches every day because, well, I guess he can't believe his fortune or his luck. Not that Grandpa's really lucky or fortunate. Not that a bunch of fish swimming around a fire pond is something you count on.

"That one's big as a railroad tie!" he'll shout to me, if I'm walking with him, which I do, especially since Grandma died.

"At least," I answer.

"I don't go in for exaggerating and you know that.

Don't need to when they're this beautiful big. But you're my witness, just in case someone doubts."

Rainbow's the only fish that Grandpa will eat. "No other fish worth catching, neither," he says. Me, I like tuna fish better. (Only fish Mom and Dad love is the perch on those all-you-can-eat nights at the lodge.) I like trawling for bluefish, too, which I've done twice, on visits with Mom's family in Maryland. So I think I like what all the fish mean to Grandpa more than what the fish mean to me. Mainly, it's cool to watch their shiny bodies darting like the sun's shine on the water, only under.

The day the Allegheny floods, all hell breaks loose. That's how Grandpa calls it: "See, even that devil creature is loose." And he means the rattlers, which take to moving from the riverbanks toward higher ground near Salamanca. They're hanging from the elderberries along the road. Who even knew snakes could drown.

Every house I visit is filled with rainwater to the doors—inside and outside. Creek water. Pond water. Lots of farms are worse than ours, but to see our place, it looks like another country, like you're looking down from an airplane and seeing these islands in an ocean— like Hawaii—except it's all just our two hundred acres. Our whole farm is all pond except for the stables across the road, and the highest spots in the meadow, and the animal buildings, which were built on higher ground just for a time like now that was never supposed to happen. The fire pond connects with the creeks, and it's deep enough for powerboats, and there are some, too, trying to save the washed-away things—ours, and stuff from nearby houses—that float or bob to the surface. So much lost and stranded livestock, too, that take weeks to return to their farms. And drowned ones, too.

Over and over Mom says things like, "No matter what we lost, we're still blessed."

As for the rainbows, they're spilled like oil spots down the highway.

It's hard to know if any are left in our pond when the water recedes—when the banks of the fire pond are where I remember them, when the rain stops long enough to pump the water from the buildings. We start two lists: what's been ruined or lost, and what can be salvaged. It's months, really, before the house feels dry, and then the winter cold seeps in, freezing all that extra water into frost and ice—at least, that's how it feels.

It's more months before the check arrives from the insurance people, which doesn't pay for hardly anything, and the check from the state and federal governments on account of our being declared a disaster area. Almost every day I remember some little thing I used to have and didn't realize the flood had swept it away. But our damages are minor compared with some people we meet, compared with families in Knapp Creek, or nearer the Allegheny.

With the start of winter, the fire pond's dark gets lighter and lighter as ice heals over the surface like a scar. No one goes there much. We just stare at the pond and it stares back—that is, when it isn't covered with fresh snow. I hardly skate at all. A few times at my friend Troy's pond. But it's like I've lost my appetite for skating or for the pond, but I don't know if that's possible. As for Grandpa, he has no reason to trudge through the drifts and walk to the pond. He heads to North Carolina for a month to visit his sister. And he spends two weeks in Atlanta, staying with Uncle Miles and his family. And the other thing is, Grandpa comes back tired, though vacations are supposed to be for rest.

Around about Mother's Day, it's finally warm enough for Grandpa to stock the pond again, even though Dad tries to suggest in a nice way that maybe the pond's better left on its own. Grandpa won't hear of that. A truck arrives with fingerlings I can't believe will grow as large as the rainbows we lost. Same day, Grandpa calls Angela and the butcher to start saving up treats for his fish. And that night, after dinner, out of the clear blue, Grandpa reaches into his shirt pocket as he leaves the table, and places his driver's license beside the centerpiece like he's presenting us with the check. "I'm done driving," he says, and then he points to me: "You'll need a car soon anyway."

He's already out of the room when Mom and Dad are saying things like, don't be silly, and why on earth, and Pop, come back in here.

Come to find out from Uncle Miles, Grandpa's had an accident—just a fender bender—in Atlanta. Afterward, he insisted on going to an optometrist or ophthalmologist—whatever—who told him he had the eyes of a teenager. He did suggest glasses to help reduce the glare at night. But as soon as he got home, Grandpa decided he wasn't going out on the road. "First and last accident in my life," he said, when we tried to talk some sense into him, which is something only Grandma could do—and once in a blue moon, she could actually succeed. It's a year before I can get my license.

Early summer's one of the driest on record, but the pond's its normal size. Except for sleeping later than six o'clock, which is when I get up for morning chores during school, I do what work everyone else does: putting in the crops, mowing, moving the animals out to pasture and back in, repairing the grain auger and the tractors with Dad. Most of my school friends do the same at their farms, and after supper, we meet at the quarry to swim or bike over to DeWitt's for ice cream.

In no time flat it's halfway through summer vacation, August first. Grandpa is reading after the rest of us are in bed. He reads more than he sleeps at night. "Don't much like closing my eyes," he says. "At my age, seeing's a kind of being proud." So Grandpa goes to make some tea, and he sees smoke rising near the barn. If he'd been asleep—if it hadn't been a clear night with an almost full moon—I don't see how any one of us would be alive now.

Grandpa shouts as he runs up the stairs. He pounds on our bedroom doors. He's the one who phones the head firefighter from Hinsdale—they're the closest, still about twelve minutes away—and they start the chain of calls to rally the volunteers and summon Mr. Tyler at the general store to sound the siren, which we can't hear from here, but I know is blaring from when I bike near town.

Until they come, there's just the four of us, and Mrs. Collins and her son, Dean, who live across the road. We all know what to do though, as if we've had fire drills every month, like at school. We start moving the animals, and then the machines. It's like a parade marching out into the middle of the field, but jumbled and scattered and in the dark. The cows and pigs are so frightened, they'd trample a person without even knowing it.

When the volunteers from Hinsdale arrive, it's no one but Grandpa who drags the fire truck's pump hose to the pond and lowers it, hand over hand, like an anchor. Even these new fish have learned the sound of his boots on the dock, the scattering of food on the water that follows. From faraway as the front yard, I can see how the glassy surface of the moonlight shatters into ripples by the dock where the rainbows are chomping at the empty air.

I help strap the Indian fire pumps on a few of the volunteers, and they join the truck at the barn to do what they can. The fire's already spread to the corn crib, where Grandpa's stationed himself.

Now, after a whole year, Grandpa will laugh if someone makes a joke about the fire. "If only we'd have grown *popping* corn, the fire would have popped enough corn to serve all the whole crowd! Hell, it looked like a drive-in movie with all those cars." But that night, the dried field-corn burns so fast and hot that the sweat steams beneath Grandpa's rubber coat—but he won't turn away except until he passes out from the heat, and the smoke, too.

A man I don't know carries Grandpa to the house, where he checks his breathing, his eyes, and his pulse. (All the volunteers—Dad's one, too—take first-aid courses.)

"Your grandpa's fine. Long as he stays inside and rests," he tells me, and *I* believe him, though Grandpa won't: He is going to catch his breath and head back out. I learn the man's name is Hawkins when he phones to tell some doctor that he's needed here.

Mom makes me stay with Grandpa. Her voice is so serious, I think even Grandpa might listen for once.

"Tell them to let the barn burn!" he orders Hawkins before he leaves the house. "No barn's going to stand on a half-burnt frame. And move the horses."

"But the stables are across the road . . ." I start to say, and then answer my own question. The twelve horses have got to be spooked. And even if they're safe for now, they'll get to panicking and kick through their stalls, break a bone or tear themselves up on the wire.

Grandpa gives me a reason I hadn't thought of. "Look out there. Too much wind."

Even though the fire's around the other side, from the back door that faces the stables and the corral, I see them outlined like by moonlight, only it's orange because of the flames. I see Mom shove the gates free. She slides open the stable's door, jumping clear since the horses charge out instantly and all at once. The horses are pitch-black, but the fire's light gives them even darker shadows, however that's possible. A few horses bolt along the fence to the entrance of the meadow, and some of them leap the rails as though it weren't the fence at all that kept them here every day, but something else. We've lost a horse before, accidentally, but never all of them at once, and never in a panicking herd. But now isn't the time for asking how we'll find them. We will. People around here know us even if we are spread out far from one another.

Then there's a new sound, louder, closer than the fire. Before I can turn to ask Grandpa the question, he tells me, "It's all right," which suddenly makes me think it's not. A spray of water bursts on the picture window. The jet runs across the wall and back, back and forth, across and back, as though it were erasing something.

"That means the house's caught fire?" I ask.

"No, no. Just preventing it," he says, but his voice is too faint; it's a whisper like a part of the farm already gone up in smoke.

Which makes me say and ask at the same time (that has to be possible): "Grandpa, we're going to be okay."

His nodding means yes and at the same time I don't know.

The one hose pounds the roof and wall and doesn't stop. It's like our own storm: one thunderbolt rumbling right against the house, but more like heat lightning since it's bright in all the windows. Water pours down the panes in sheets, and the view is blurred and wobbly, like looking through the sheer curtains when the window's cracked open in Grandpa's room. But even so, I know what's out there: I watch the embers float, slower than pennies in a wishing well, from the barn to the stables, to the milk house, to the grain elevator that's thirty-six feet tall—the tallest thing for miles—and over to one and then the other silo.

Behind me, from the couch where Grandpa's supposed to be lying still, I hear him talking like he's talking to the rainbows, or like he's giving directions and he's still out there fighting the flames. I can see the fire outside in his eyes, which must mean it's reflected in my eyes, too, if Grandpa looks up to see it.

"The pond's not deep enough," Grandpa tells me, as if he'd just remembered how deep they'd dug it. I bring him some juice from the fridge. I don't know why I can't be doing something more than watching Grandpa—though if I weren't here, he wouldn't be either.

There's so much light, I keep forgetting it's night. Besides the flames, there's the white flash of cameras: someone from the insurance company and a photographer for the *Journal*. And probably people just wanting to shoot some cool pictures. And then, even at the farther-away dark edges, there are yellower lights, and red ones—new ones: headlights and taillights of cars pulling in. (The *Journal*, which only comes out once a week, will say that two thousand people attended the fire—drove from nearby towns like we were some kind of county fair that opened after midnight. There should have been another story to say how people kept coming for days—not thousands, but more than just people we know by name—strangers coming to drop off things they had extra of, like a milking machine or a bridle, and, of course, things to eat, as though the fire had burned the kitchen, too, but it didn't—only whatever it is inside a person that's supposed to make us want to eat or want to wake up.)

When I crack the front door just to see something clearly, a burst of smoke slips in before my eyes can really make out much.

"Seems like maybe there's even more firemen now, Grandpa," I tell him, and he nods, as though he'd been calculating how long it'd take the volunteers from each of the neighboring villages to make their way here.

"Probably. Probably be at least three fire trucks by now." And then, after too long a pause, he finishes. "Look at it go. Fire's just like trout heading upstream: slow and certain of where it's going."

That's when Mom comes in again with one of the cats, bringing not only the smell but also the heat of the fire in her clothes and hair. She confirms what Grandpa guessed: "There's three trucks pumping water now. And so many other people wanting to help, they've got two men just keeping the crowd back." Her eyes leak tears down her cheek—maybe it's just from the smoke—her talk has more important things to do than sob. We fill bottles and jugs of water at the sink to take to the fire-fighters.

The seven thousand hay bales blaze all night, glowing right alongside the dawn, when all that's left of the barn is an arch that frames the sunrise. It's quiet, then, suddenly, like an alarm clock went off, but one that wakes you with silence since the night was so loud. The firemen coil their hoses half-filled with pond sludge, and the last of the crowds drive home to Portville, Ischua, and Knapp Creek.

Friends in Olean, and farther south than Hinsdale, smell the smoke at sunup, the dead fish at dusk. The phone is always ringing. One call is from the Luthers, who have managed to pen the four horses that escaped. They'll hold them as long as we need them to.

It's three days before the coals lose heat, before Mom and Dad are done meeting the insurance people and the county agents. Grandpa and I comb the property after supper. The machines are still clustered in the pasture like cows, as though the only job they had was to wait. Since nothing else stands but the house and the woods—and the stables across the road, which were unharmed, after all—we watch the ground as if something were left here and we had to come to look. Instead of grass or dirt it's ashes, wet wherever we step. Across the meadow where the fire pond was, there's a mud valley now that's like a mirage of water, shimmering the way a highway in the summer heat looks wet until you get closer and see it's not. The pond shimmers, but closer up, it's the silt rippling where the tails are flaring beneath.

When Grandpa takes off his shoes and socks, I take off mine. We set them on the dock and climb down to the muck of the bottom. Forty years ago, I think to myself, Grandpa stood on the bottom like this.

We start off walking, our feet sinking into the clay, then popping free with a suction sound.

"It's raining," Grandpa announces to me, or maybe he's just used to talking to himself at the pond. He's smiling, even though no amount of water—not from clouds, not from our springs or our well, not from tanker trucks with nothing better to do than to cart water here— nothing will save the rainbows. The ones at the shallow end are dead. These last few that move have already drowned in the air.

Grandpa says, "I already hear them talking."

"Who, Grandpa?" I ask. I know he doesn't mean the fish.

"Just people. I hear them. 'You'd think that old fool'd have learnt that first time never to stock a fire pond.'"

"No, they're not, Grandpa," I answer him, "they won't," though this is just another thing I don't know. I don't know if Grandpa's thinking about restocking the pond, or if I should plead with him not to if only so he'll slap me hard enough to let me cry. I don't know even why I think this, because he'd never do that.

"I'm going to tell you something," he says, "and I don't care if you're old enough to think you should start ignoring advice."

I do know I should tell him I'm not, that I'm listening, to go ahead, to keep walking—*something*. So I take a step forward. Grandpa's planted there like he's a boot that just slipped off your foot and stuck there. So I have to step back.

"You stock your life with what all makes you happy, you hear me? You put rainbows anyplace you like, not excepting your young heart."

And then it's Grandpa who turns, ready to complete our tour, if that's what we're doing, drawing a circle with footstep dashes around the fire pond like it's something you could cut out. But before I can say anything like I'm sorry or I believe you, he adds: "I'm not expecting you to answer."

Grandpa's footprints are the size of mine (the size of the fingerlings—grown a lot, of course, since May): They're little ponds the coming rain will fill, then flood, then wash away.

A Note From the Author

In 1977, heading toward my first writer's conference,
I visited the home of the fellow student with whom I
was ride-sharing. This was upstate New York, rolling
countryside with grainfields and livestock, a landscape I
knew from Sunday drives we took as children, leaving our
new suburb of Columbus, Ohio. At one point my colleague's
father showed me news clippings of the day their farm
had all but burned to the ground. (Maybe it was the
grandfather. Fictionalizing an experience changes it
so thoroughly, so permanently, I often can't distinguish
the passing facts from my own memorizing revisions.)

He described how the small pond they'd dug on
the property had been drained by the firefighters. I'd never
heard of a fire pond, I'd never guessed how rural homes
without fire hydrants could channel water to the hoses.

Other hardships wove into the family's memories
of the fire: an earlier flood, crop failures, illnesses, financial
trouble. But one seemingly trivial addition somehow took
this blunt narration of recent tragedies and sharpened it,
wounding me so that I could feel a wince of the family's

grief. They had stocked their fire pond with trout. And just as their own fates had been twisted with these disasters, so, too, had the fates of their fish.

Eventually I wrote a poem for my first collection that focused on the trout. But for almost twenty-five more years, a larger story lay fallow, one that reinvented the grandfather as well as this fictional child that, I suppose, I've inserted to help imagine how my own curious, aghast, overly sensitive self might have responded.

I possess no greater compassion for animals than I do for humans. But I suffer, as many of us do, from feeling overwhelmed by the news of abuses, crimes, atrocities, and devastation. Subconsciously, I build up some callousness that allows me to keep working or eating or writing, instead of despairing at these sufferings. Yet, at times, animals release the emotions beneath this shielding. In this story, the trout did this. Animals, in life and in writing, sometimes allow me a way to admit that greater empathy. They are a way in. They are a way out.

Is this because animals are such bystanders, such innocents in the crises we humans often create? Is it because animals have little voice to complain or to accuse, no way to understand the rationalizations we all too often accept? Is it because animals—at least, the ones who share our homes—give us a chance to understand our own animal natures?

The things that happened in "The Fire Pond" did not happen to me. But what-the-things-felt-like-to-the-people-in-the-story, those indeed happened to me as I wrote the story and chanced to remember events in my own life. I hope, after reading this story of things that did not happen to you, either, something in your own experience made you remember what-the-things-felt-like.

I now live in the countryside. There's a fire pond, stocked with bass and panfish, for a day that I hope will never arise. Although I still fear it, I have already imagined it. When a story reaches its full potential, it can help in this way: It can inoculate us, so that we can meet the worst that is to come with a little immunity, a little reserve for fighting hopelessness.

CHAIR
A Story for Voices

VIRGINIA EUWER WOLFF

Voices:
BUDDY
GRANDPA

I
Happy Birthday, Buddy

GRANDPA: Happy Birthday, Buddy. Are you ready?
BUDDY: Sure.
GRANDPA: Well, sit right down in that chair over there. You know I made that chair.
BUDDY: Yes, I know, Grandpa.
GRANDPA: That's old oak, that tree was 128 feet, 11 inches tall, it blew down in the storm of '53. Right in the front yard. Your dad said, "Hey, there's a tree across the porch!" I made that chair over the winter. I worked on it every night.
BUDDY: It's a nice chair, Grandpa. I don't know

anybody else who can sit in a chair made by his great-grandfather.

GRANDPA: I made every bit of it. It's never creaked, the legs have never loosened, it's never given up. Every piece fits. Nothing unnecessary in that chair.

BUDDY: It's a good chair, Grandpa. You did a great job on it.

GRANDPA: Your father helped a little bit with the sanding. He was impatient, always wanting to be out and about. But he helped a little. You're not like your dad. You're more heartful. Remember when you took in that stray cat? The striped one?

BUDDY: It died.

GRANDPA: The point is you saved it once. You couldn't save it forever. You've always been a go-getter. Always asking things: "How do they get the rings to go around a raccoon's eyes?" "Why don't the quills hurt the porcupine?" "How does the telephone know our number?" Well, here we go. Pay attention. Look at birds. Climb mountains. Spend a night in a desert. See the ocean repeat itself and yet never repeat itself. Note eclipses. Watch rain. Don't put your faith in banks. Never spit out of a car window.

BUDDY: Spit out of a car window? Why would I want to do that?

GRANDPA: You wouldn't. I'm just telling you. Never do it.

BUDDY: I won't.

GRANDPA: I'm just telling you. People do it. It's a terrible thing. Spreads germs. It's rude. It insults the rest of us. We're decent people. I would never do that if I lived nine hundred years.

BUDDY: I know you wouldn't, Grandpa.

GRANDPA: I'm just telling you. Never do it. Blast it, you don't want to be the kind of person spits out of a car window.

BUDDY: I don't know anybody who spits out of car windows.

GRANDPA: Yes, you do. You just don't *know* they spit out of car windows.

BUDDY: Maybe so.

GRANDPA: For sure so. I'm telling you. Would I lie to you?

BUDDY: I don't think so.

GRANDPA: You don't think so? You don't *think* so?

BUDDY: What if you've lied to me but I haven't found out about it?

GRANDPA: When have I ever lied to you?

BUDDY: That's what I'm saying. I don't know.

GRANDPA: You don't trust me?

BUDDY: I do trust you. I've trusted you all my life.

GRANDPA: Then why do you think I've lied to you?

BUDDY: I don't.

GRANDPA: Well then.

BUDDY: I'd never spit out of a car window.

GRANDPA: Ha.

BUDDY: What else do you have for me?

GRANDPA: Scrutinize your motives. Shape your arguments. Let the light in. But the dark is good, too. In the dark is where you learn about fear. Don't be squeamish.

BUDDY: I'm not sure I understand all this.

GRANDPA: Of course you don't. It'll take years. That is a *fine* chair you're sitting in, isn't it?

BUDDY: It sure is. How did you make the legs?

GRANDPA: With a saw. With a chisel. With a lathe. With sandpaper. With care. With precision. With time.

BUDDY: You know, I look like you, Grandpa. When you were young. My mom and dad think so, and I can tell, too. From pictures. That one of you just home from the Korean War.

GRANDPA: What do you have this year?

BUDDY: Soccer, math, the guys. Piano. Science fiction. Computer.

GRANDPA: How fast can you put those in alphabetical order?

BUDDY: Uh. Computer, the guys, math, piano, science fiction, soccer.

GRANDPA: How fast can you put them in order of importance?

BUDDY: What kind of importance? Importance to me, or in the world or what?

GRANDPA: Importance in the big picture.

BUDDY: Oh. Uh. Math? Soccer? Computer, then the guys, then science fiction. Piano?

GRANDPA: Well, you're still young. You'll think it over.

BUDDY: I have thought it over.

GRANDPA: Not much.

BUDDY: Do you think I don't know *any*thing?

GRANDPA: You don't know much. Understand why we fight wars. Notice why government doesn't work. Observe how science and religion pick childish fights with each other. Learn about history. Error and greed: the life story of the human race, blast it. Don't hurt the ones you love. Don't hurt the ones you don't love, either. Do you still want to be a veterinarian?

BUDDY: No, now I want to be a helicopter pilot.

GRANDPA: Well. That's all right, too. Just don't forget the most important thing: Be alert. Be attentive. Spend a whole day thinking about sorrow. Spend a day thinking about joy.

BUDDY: How do you mean?

GRANDPA: Don't worry. The opportunities will present themselves. You just have to be awake when they come to your doorstep.

BUDDY: I don't think I get it.

GRANDPA: Consider the galaxies. Go without clocks and watches one day a week. That's not too much to ask of yourself. You'll be glad you did.

BUDDY: I already do. You told me to do that last year. And I'm late to things and people get upset.

GRANDPA: Well, do it anyway. And be polite. You can be both polite and manly. You can do that. It has been done before.

BUDDY: I try.

GRANDPA: Please and thank you aren't enough. Be considerate. Be unselfish. Even up there in the sky in a helicopter you can be considerate.

BUDDY: Okay.

GRANDPA: The meaning of life will find you.

BUDDY: How?

GRANDPA: Keep your eyes open. Enjoy the little nothing moments. While you're waiting for the fish to bite. Waiting for the water to boil. Walking through doorways. Waiting for the rain to stop, the apples to ripen, the inning to be over. Waiting for the light to turn green. Waiting for the weather to clear so you can go up in your helicopter. Little nothing moments.

BUDDY: That's how the meaning of life finds you?

GRANDPA: It comes to you little by little. Life is not a movie. You don't walk in and sit down and have somebody show it to you. It comes to you in pieces. Like pebbles. On a path to a creek. Little glimmers of light up there in the sky in your helicopter. And another thing: Think very hard before you decide to give your life for your country.

BUDDY: I don't know anything I'd give my life for.

GRANDPA: That's because you haven't learned to care enough about anything. My father, Franklin, died for a country you haven't begun to appreciate yet. In France, 1918.

BUDDY: Why?

GRANDPA: So you could live free and grow strong and have a life, Buddy. That's why. So you could have a life.

BUDDY: I don't think I see the connection. That was France.

GRANDPA: Be a necessary man, Buddy. Be a man the world needs.

BUDDY: Grandpa, you've got a mind that won't quit.

II
Happy Birthday, Buddy

GRANDPA: Happy Birthday, Buddy.

BUDDY: Thank you.

GRANDPA: I wondered when you'd begin to say that. I've been waiting a long time.

BUDDY: I didn't say it last year?

GRANDPA: Definitely not.

BUDDY: I wonder why.

GRANDPA: That's what we spend our whole lives doing. Wondering why we did or didn't do things. Scrutinizing our motives. Like I told you before. "The unexamined life is not worth living." Socrates said that. You ready?

BUDDY: Sure.

GRANDPA: So. You broke your ankle in soccer.

BUDDY: Yeah.

GRANDPA: And you got third place in the piano contest.

BUDDY: Yeah. I don't like to practice.

GRANDPA: Do you like music?

BUDDY: Yes.

GRANDPA: Then practice. What do you have this year?

BUDDY: Soccer. Science. A girlfriend, sort of. Math. Piano. The guys.

GRANDPA: A girlfriend, "sort of"? What does that mean?

BUDDY: I mean I don't know. I don't know if she likes me. I think she does. Maybe she doesn't.

GRANDPA: Story of life on Earth. Sit right over there in that oak chair. You know I made that chair in the winter of 1953?

BUDDY: Yes. I know you did. And my dad said, "There's a tree across the yard."

GRANDPA: "Across the porch." It was sprawled clear across the doorway. Nobody could get in or out till we sawed it up. I made that chair, it took me a whole winter to finish it. Nothing unnecessary in that chair.

BUDDY: And my dad helped.

GRANDPA: That's right. Edward didn't help much, but Paul did.

BUDDY: I thought you said my dad helped.

GRANDPA: I did say that. Paul didn't help much, but Edward did.

BUDDY: That's not what you said.

GRANDPA: Don't tell me what I said.

BUDDY: I mean this time. That's what you said last year. But just now you said, "Edward didn't help much, but Paul did." Edward is my dad. Paul is my grandfather. You're my great-grandfather.

GRANDPA: Don't tell me who's who in this family. I ought to know. I know who helped me make that chair and who didn't. Do you still want to be a helicopter pilot?

BUDDY: No, I want to be a chemist.

GRANDPA: Well, that's all right, too. Just remember the important things: Get to know Plato. Confucius. Rembrandt. Waterfalls. Logarithms. Beethoven. Australia. Eggs.

BUDDY: How do I do that all at once?

GRANDPA: You don't do it all at once. You do it a little bit at a time, Buddy.

BUDDY: Grandpa, how do you know when you *know* something?

GRANDPA: You follow the dots. Check the cellar and the attic.

BUDDY: Of the house?

GRANDPA: Of your life. And check under your skin.

BUDDY: Why?

GRANDPA: To see what's gotten under there.

BUDDY: I don't think I'm following you, Grandpa.

GRANDPA: Grandpa isn't here. He died in France, fighting the Germans. 1918. He was a necessary man and he died in the Great War. Nothing like it before or since.

BUDDY: I meant *you* when I said "Grandpa," Grandpa.

GRANDPA: I'm not your grandpa. Your grandpa is dead in France, 1918.

BUDDY: No, that's *your* father.

GRANDPA: Well. Anyway. Be prepared to eat your words.

BUDDY: Do I have to?

GRANDPA: Sure you do. Because you're going to be wrong.

BUDDY: You were wrong back there.

GRANDPA: Back there when I made that chair, I was right, all right. That chair. It's endurance. That's what it is.

BUDDY: It's what *what* is?

GRANDPA: The puzzle. The ammunition. The fences. The school. The decision. All of it.

BUDDY: Endurance. Okay. Yeah, it's good to have endurance.

GRANDPA: Know the basics. Knowledge isn't power unless it's sheltered in wisdom. The necessary man has wisdom. Be a necessary man.

BUDDY: How can I do everything you're telling me to do?

GRANDPA: You will wonder why you aren't happy. You will wonder if you are happy.

BUDDY: How can you be so sure?

GRANDPA: I've lived a long time and I'm sure. The quiet desperation is what you need to be prepared for.

BUDDY: How do I get prepared for that?

GRANDPA: I haven't a clue.

BUDDY: What about encouragement?

GRANDPA: What about it?

BUDDY: Well . . .

GRANDPA: There's your answer. In a breath. In a wink. Here and gone.

BUDDY: You don't make me feel very hopeful.

GRANDPA: Oh, was I supposed to make you feel very hopeful? Listen, Buddy: It's the continual hammering of the heart. *That's* what it is. The mind may eventually be understood. But the human heart? Never.

BUDDY: Then what's the point of trying?

GRANDPA: Ha.

BUDDY: Grandpa, I don't get some of this.

GRANDPA: You would never spit out of a car window, would you?

BUDDY: No, I wouldn't.

GRANDPA: Believe me, people do it. More people than you think.

BUDDY: I believe you.

GRANDPA: You get old, you become unnecessary. An unnecessary man. It's a terrible thing.

BUDDY: That'll never happen to you, Grandpa. You've got enough endurance to last you a long, long time.

III
Happy Birthday, Buddy

BUDDY: It's my birthday, Grandpa.

GRANDPA: Up here. All of it's up here, son.

BUDDY: I'm not your son. My grandfather Paul is your son. His son is my father, Edward. I'm Edward's son, Buddy.

GRANDPA: You ever spit out of a car window?

BUDDY: Never. Aren't you going to ask me what I have this year? I made a goal in soccer last week.

GRANDPA: Rice Krispies. Get them all over.

BUDDY: Huh? You should see my science experiment. It's got tubes and wheels and it lights up—

GRANDPA: All over. Done with. Nowhere.

BUDDY: I've decided I want to study gene patterns. Can you hear me, Grandpa?

GRANDPA: Logic. That's what. No logic. Rice Krispies.

BUDDY: Grandpa, I have chemistry this year. I have a different girlfriend now. And I have math and computer. And I'm still practicing the piano.

GRANDPA: Forest and trees. Not anymore.

BUDDY: Grandpa, try to concentrate. Let me tell you about—

GRANDPA: Without Grandpa. He died Fromany 18. He isn't here to be.

BUDDY: I don't get you.

GRANDPA: Get ness. Get ness.

BUDDY: I'd get it for you if I could. I just don't know what you want.

GRANDPA: Ness.

BUDDY: What?

GRANDPA: Ness. Ness. *Ness*, blast it. Ness. NESS.

BUDDY: I wish I knew what you meant, Grandpa.

GRANDPA: Ness. Un. Un. Un. Un. Ness. Ness. Air.
Ness air. Ness. Air.

BUDDY: I'm confused.

GRANDPA: Ness. Un. Ness air.

BUDDY: Can you give me a hint?

GRANDPA: Man. Un ness. Blast it. Man.

BUDDY: What's going on, Grandpa?

GRANDPA: Speak up, Paul. Un. Ness.

BUDDY: Un. Ness. Air. Unnessair. Unnessair.
Unnecessair—unnecessary?

GRANDPA: Yeah. Yeah. Me. Un ness air.

BUDDY: Where did you go, Grandpa?

GRANDPA: Don't mumblejumble. Over there. Thing.

BUDDY: What did you say?

GRANDPA: Me. Un ness. Over there. Right over there.
Thing. Over there. Thing.

BUDDY: It's a chair, Grandpa.

A Note From the Author

*At the Whitney Museum in New York in 1999, I saw a
piece by the artist Joseph Kosuth. The work is called*
One and Three Chairs, *dates from 1965, and consists of
a rustic wooden chair, a photograph of a chair, and the
word "chair." As I looked at the three things together, I
imagined being a very young child, not yet able to read the
word. I also envisioned an elderly person having forgotten
the word. Somewhere on my three thousand-mile trip back
home, flying high above the clouds, this interesting
situation must have combined with some notes I'd made
several years before. The notes were simply fragments of
conversation between a grandfather and grandson. These
two thoughts—the chair in the New York museum and the
notes in a drawer in Oregon—may have met while I was
napping on the airplane.*

*Then came the hard work: sculpting a story out of what
was really just a jumble of ideas.*

*One of the things that interests me most about loss is that
often, while we are being swept away by losing something,
we are gaining something else that totally surprises us.*

RED SEVEN

C. B. CHRISTIANSEN

We buried Grandma in the backyard. Daddy thought it might be against the law, but my mother, in her most fervent Italian, replied, *"Fagioli!"* Beans. The next day, we lay Grandma to rest in the orchard, beneath the ancient pear tree. When it came time to eulogize her, Daddy cleared his throat and explained. "First thing every autumn morning, Grandma headed straight to this tree to gather up the windfall pears." He cradled a handful of hanging fruit, for it was September and the tree was laden. "She ate three to four for breakfast every day," he continued. "She loved these pears. She loved this tree. It's a fitting place . . ." He stopped and blinked and wiped his eyes.

What Daddy did not say was that the pears gave Grandma gas. It wouldn't have been respectful. Besides, it was a well-known fact among the people gathered there to honor her: Grandma could clear a room with her flatulence. Even outdoors, if the breeze was right, she could cause a mass migration to fresher air.

Daddy was too tearful to continue. Uncle Rev, my mother's bachelor brother, concluded the speaking part of the service. "Truly, she will not pass this way again."

"Amen," whispered Miss Olivia Meadowbrook, one of Grandma's admirers. "Uh-huh!" said Paolo Pordini, and, finally, his sister, Francesca, chimed in, "Hallelujah!"

"Then again," said Uncle Rev, "I could be wrong."

We all shared a laugh, even my mother, who was heartbroken the day we buried Grandma.

My contribution to the ceremony was to play "Amazing Grace" on my flute. The notes floated through the orchard and over the long table set for the feast to come. My mother cried. My father, too, for all that had led to this moment.

Before Grandma came to live with us, we plodded along the way families do, following the routines of daily life. I went to junior high school. Daddy went to work. My mother remained at the kitchen table in her bathrobe, sipping a second cup of coffee. I came home right after school to see if my mother had gotten dressed. On days she hadn't, I would make sandwiches. On the days she had, I'd do homework at the kitchen table while my mother started dinner. On more than one occasion, she cried silently over the stove.

Our unspoken rule was to see nothing, say nothing, feel nothing. One evening, as my mother cried, I watched the drops fall, sizzling, into the frying ham. *Sss. Sss. Sss.*

My job was to continue reading *The Scarlet Letter*, continue listing the major exports of Brazil, continue memorizing the periodic table of elements and its common applications. Salt: NaCl. Water: H_2O. Tears: H_2ONaCl? I ate the ham. It was salty anyway.

My mother's tears were such a part of me, I didn't know things could be different. I didn't know a girl could have friends or music or a life of her own.

My mother's good moods gradually became rare as samarium (Sm), more precious than pearls. She began to play solitaire, day and night, at the kitchen table. Daddy and I tried to cheer her up. I brought home jokes. She didn't laugh. Daddy brought home takeout. She didn't eat. We made her a hair appointment. She canceled. One night, we went to a drive-in restaurant, leaving my mother at the kitchen table with her chow mein and her deck of cards. Over bacon cheeseburgers and strawberry milk shakes, we agreed my mother wasn't herself anymore. "She needs *something*," Daddy said. "I don't know—fresh air, maybe?" His shrug was a giant question mark. I shrugged back. "And some company during the day?" I added. Daddy and I looked at each other and, at the same moment, proclaimed, "A dog!" Our question marks disappeared. "A puppy," I whispered, awed by our simultaneous solution to my mother's problem.

How could we have been so wrong?

How could we have been so right?

The next Saturday morning, we decided on a black Labrador retriever. I suppose we hoped a Lab would fetch my mother and bring her back to us. "Can we call her 'Joy'?" I asked. The study of Hawthorne had taught me a thing or two about symbolism. I wanted to bring joy into my mother's life. Was there anything wrong with that? "It suits her," said Daddy, "but it's up to your mother, don't you think?" Reluctantly, I agreed.

When I carried the furry bundle of energy into the kitchen, my mother burst into tears. The puppy took a long look at my mother and began to cry, too. Daddy and I glanced at each other in alarm. This wasn't the introduction we had imagined over bacon cheeseburgers. I set the puppy at my feet. She wouldn't budge. Neither would my mother. The kitchen clock ticked loudly. Finally, mercifully, some primitive maternal instinct took over, and my mother got down on the floor. The puppy stopped crying immediately. On stubby legs, she took three steps toward my mother's outstretched hand. Her tiny tail wagged in a furious circle. Ah. *This* was how I'd pictured their meeting. The puppy took another step and she stopped and she squatted and she peed on the floor. We all watched the puddle spread in an ever-widening circle. They both started howling again. And there was morning and there was evening on the first day.

The puppy cried all night.

"Take her back," my mother said. Somehow we never got around to it. So every morning, my mother got up at six A.M. to feed the barking puppy and take her outside to go potty. "Fresh air?" Daddy said to me hopefully. My mother slept another fitful hour on the small kitchen couch while the dog played tug-of-war with her bathrobe tie. "Company?" I wondered aloud to my father. My mother refused to name the dog "Joy" or anything else. She called her the *&$#! puppy.

Life lurched on.

The *&$#! puppy favored Daddy and me with sloppy kisses and nuzzling, nipping puppy games. But she made it her mission to annoy my mother. Every time my mother tried to play solitaire, the *&$#! puppy barked for attention. She got underfoot, constantly causing her to stumble. She peed on the newspapers my mother set down (good) about a hundred times a day (not so good). "Normal puppy behaviors," Daddy and I assured each other. But even we couldn't ignore the staring. The *&$#! puppy's wise brown eyes followed my mother everywhere. "It's driving me crazy," my mother said. We thought she was joking.

We were eating sandwiches for dinner one Sunday in September when the *&$#! puppy pranced into the kitchen. She carried a terry cloth sleeve that she had industriously detached from the body of my mother's bathrobe. My mother raised an accusing finger. "I do everything for you," she shouted, "and you treat me like dirt!" The *&$#! puppy cocked her head and wedged her brows together, confused. She looked adorable. My mother began to laugh. Daddy and I grinned. We hadn't heard my mother laugh in ages. She laughed and laughed. When she didn't stop, our grins disappeared. I covered my ears. It was worse than the crying.

I think it scared her, that uncontrollable laughter, because afterward, my mother tried to structure her life around her daily to-do lists. Three things a day were as much as she could manage. Uncle Rev said the lists probably gave her a sense of control: vacuum, reattach bathrobe sleeve, take care of the dog; scrub kitchen floor, sharpen knives, take care of the dog; buy shovel, scoop poop, take care of the dog. Such bleak lists. No friends, no music, no life of her own.

But Daddy said he thought things were getting better. And life was predictable around our house until one late September afternoon. When I came home right after school to check on her, my mother was not in her usual place in the kitchen. A game of solitaire was spread out over the table. She had dealt a winning hand. The reds and blacks formed alternating patterns in four straight columns. I wondered how she had managed to complete the game with the *&$#! puppy vying for her attention. Where were they anyway? I searched the downstairs. No luck. Back in the kitchen, beneath the ace of spades, I found that day's to-do list: end this misery, call the vet, take care of the dog.

"Puppy?" I whispered. My voice shook. There was no sign of Joy. I crept upstairs, feeling stupidly hopeful. The *&$#! puppy had never been allowed upstairs.

I heard my mother's soft murmur coming from my parents' bedroom, but I hesitated to move closer. Then I heard Daddy's voice. "You didn't!" he said. "Tell me you didn't!" My ear was against their door in a flash. "I knew you were having a hard time, but I had no idea it was this bad. It never occurred to me that you would contemplate . . ."

". . . ending the misery?" my mother finished.

Though I felt like running, I stood frozen at the door.

There was only one conclusion to be drawn from my parents' conversation, but I hoped if I kept listening, I would be proven wrong.

"It sounds so melodramatic now," my mother continued, "but that solitaire game was really a matter of life or death. And I won. I won . . ."

I waited for more. There was silence, and then all I could hear was Daddy crying.

I sank to the floor, the weight of my understanding too heavy to bear. My mind filled with images of my mother's accusing finger, her lists of shovels and sharpened knives and unspeakable arrangements with the vet. End this misery. Take care of the dog. What awful chain of events had Daddy and I set in motion that night at the drive-in restaurant? We had taken that innocent puppy from her cozy litter and plunked her down in this stale house of woe. Now she was gone, her deep, wise eyes closed forever.

I buried my face in my hands and wept to think my mother had put an end to Joy. What kind of person would do a thing like that? I don't know how long I cried. But suddenly my mother was patting my back. I pulled away. Her touch made my stomach churn. I thought I might be sick all over the carpet and wouldn't *that* upset my mother's rigid little world?

"Things are going to be better now," she said calmly. She knew I'd heard everything, but she didn't even sound sorry! I hated her. I hated our whole dismal existence. I raised my face to tell her so, to spew every ounce of anger and worry I'd been feeling, but before I could open my mouth, I was bombarded by a black blur. I heard an eager snuffling. A soft, quick tongue licked away my tears. I was kissed by Joy. I was overcome by Joy. Joy wiggled in my arms and peed all over the front of me. When the warm flood leaked onto the carpet, I looked at my mother's face expecting anger, expecting resignation, expecting tolerance, expecting anything but what I saw there.

What I saw there was the truth: It wasn't the *&$#! puppy's life my mother had contemplated ending. It was her own.

We didn't talk about it. I knew. She knew I knew. What was there to say? Quietly, secretly, I began keeping a household inventory of razor blades, pills, ropes, pesticides. I was suspicious of anything that could hurt my mother. Or rather, anything with which my mother could hurt herself. Toothpicks. Thumbtacks. Duct tape. (I had a rich imagination.) At the same time, I experienced an odd sense of relief, the kind a girl might feel after putting the last piece of a puzzle in place. It completed a picture I didn't want to see, but at least it fit. Deep inside, I knew my mother had ended her life long ago. If she was going to live, I wanted her to *live*. I had spent years trying to cheer her up. What more could I do?

She tried to reassure me. "Things are going to be better now," she said again and again. I was skeptical, but I kept it to myself. My mother went to three different doctors and a naturopath. She tried medication, mediation, meditation. Finally, she threw away her bathrobe and got dressed in the mornings and I began to believe her.

Of course, as my mother took over the job of making herself happy, I was left with less and less to do.

I still came home right after school every day to watch over her. But more often than not, I found my mother busy in the garden. The *&$#! puppy (my mother now called her "the puppy," for short) romped through the overgrown orchard. One day, I came home and they were both gone. "Gone for a walk to the nursery," the note said. "Back before dinner." I sat at the kitchen table, waiting. I didn't have homework that day. I wasn't hungry. I wasn't thirsty. I wasn't sleepy. I was bored. No, it was more complicated than boredom. I was empty. I drummed my fingers on the table. I walked around the room. I opened cupboards and drawers and even the oven, looking for something to fill the emptiness. In the corner of one drawer I found my mother's deck of cards. I shuffled them over and over, the sound exploding in my ears. I dealt them out in the careful pattern my mother had taught me. As I played them, reds on blacks, aces on top, I began to understand why my mother liked this game. Creating order out of chaos gives a girl the illusion of control. Red king, black queen, jack of diamonds, black ten, red nine, eight of clubs. And . . . I flipped through the cards. Nope, nope, nope. It wasn't in my hand. I was stuck. I was frustrated. I needed one card, just to keep going. I found it hidden in one of the piles on the table. This was worse. I could see what I needed, but even though it was within my reach, I couldn't take it.

The back door opened and the puppy skittered across

the floor to me. My mother followed, cheeks rosy, arms filled with brand-new pruners and a trowel and a box of bonemeal. When she saw me playing solitaire, she dropped everything with a clatter that sent the puppy scurrying under the table. "Are you all right?" she asked softly.

I guess I wasn't all right. I had thought I was empty but, in fact, I was full of NaCl and H_2O. My tears flowed out and down my face and onto my mother's cards. She wrapped her arms around me while the puppy cried along from under the table. "Shhh," my mother said. "*Shhh. Shhh. Shhh.*" But I had to tell her. "I'm stuck," I said "I can't go forward and I can't go backward." My mother patted my back. Her touch calmed me enough to blurt, "All I needed was the red seven!" Even as I said it, it sounded like the dumbest comment in the whole wide world, but my mother took my face in her hands and looked me in the eye and said, "I know. Oh, honey, I know."

Then my mother called her bachelor brother, my beloved Uncle Rev. That night we sat in the living room by the fire—Daddy, Uncle Rev, my mother, myself, and the puppy (who was now allowed to roam wherever she pleased). Uncle Rev sipped his coffee and ate a cookie and told me the story of Grandma.

"Grandma came to live with us after her husband died."

The puppy sighed and rested her chin on her little forepaws.

Uncle Rev bent to scratch her ears. "She was never the cheeriest 'O' in the box, but she was kind and gentle and wise. I think it was the smell thing that finally did her in."

"Smell?" I asked.

"She lost her sense of smell," said my mother. "One day she could smell roses, peanut butter, garbage in the pail. The next day, she stuck her face into a can of ground coffee and said, 'Nothing. I smell nothing.'"

As if she couldn't sit still for such a story, the puppy stood to run her nose across the carpet like a self-propelled vacuum cleaner.

"The doctors thought it was caused by some sort of infection," my mother said.

"After that, Grandma took to her bed and rarely got up," added Uncle Rev.

"She must have been so sad," I said. I breathed in wood smoke and the clean perfume of my mother's hair and a faint scent of ginger from the plate of cookies set on the mantle, safe from the puppy.

"She *was* sad," said Uncle Rev. "And she had reason to be. It's just that some people get over things. And she never did. When Grandma didn't get better, Mother got sad. Later, I found out depression runs in our family. Or should I say, it creeps like mud. Some of us fight our way through it every day. Some of us are caught up in its downhill progression. And some of us stand help-lessly by, watching, as the ones we love are slowly swept under."

"Why are you telling *me* this?"

"Somehow Mother managed to raise us and nurture us. And Grandma always said she loved us more than life itself, but . . ."

"But what?"

My mother touched my hair. "It took a lot out of us, trying to make her happy enough to get out of bed. I remember how it was. I don't want you to carry that kind of burden any longer."

"And you don't have to!" said Uncle Rev.

The puppy planted herself at my mother's feet and nudged her with her nose. My mother stroked her on the top of her little black snout. The puppy sniffed my mother's hand.

"Some of us get a second chance," said Uncle Rev. "Like your mother."

"But not Grandma," I said.

The puppy stopped sniffing and looked up at my mother with her wise, brown eyes. My mother's own eyes widened in surprise.

"Not Grandma," said Uncle Rev.

The puppy barked. "Rowf!"

"Potty?" asked Daddy helpfully, but my mother held up her hand.

"Grandma," she said.

The puppy barked again. "Rowf!"

"Grandma?"

"ROWF!"

"Grandma!" my mother said. "Are *you* . . . ?"

"Aw, sis . . . ," began Uncle Rev.

The puppy gazed steadily at my mother, waiting.

"I know it sounds crazy," said my mother, "but do you suppose she came back?"

"I really don't think . . . ," began Uncle Rev.

". . . to lead me out of the mud, I mean."

The puppy continued gazing at my mother.

"You all saw how she drove me to the edge. She forced me to get help!"

"Well, yes . . . ," Uncle Rev conceded, "but . . ."

"You know, she has an incredible sense of smell," bragged my mother, as if she'd loved the *&$#! puppy all along. "I think she came back so she could sniff to her heart's content."

"Rowf! Rowf! Rowf!" The puppy nearly danced with glee.

Uncle Rev put on his reading glasses and leaned over to scrutinize the puppy, who, in turn, stood on her back legs to lick his face. I thought I heard him whisper, "Grammy?"

In any case, Daddy had had enough. "Puppy!" he commanded firmly, in accordance with the obedience manual. "Off!"

"Sweetheart," said my mother, "please don't use that tone with Grandma."

During the silence that followed, I realized I wasn't the only one in the family with a rich imagination. I pulled the puppy into my lap. "Congratulations, Grandma," I said. "You finally have a name."

Five years later, we buried Grandma in the backyard. It was a different garden from the weed-choked wasteland of before. Now it was filled with flowers and herbs and grapevines and climbing roses. Other plants were ripe with the memories of blueberries, strawberries, raspberries. There were fruit trees heavy with plums and apples and pears, the same pears that had given Grandma such delight and indigestion. It was the smell of those wind-fall pears that had first led Grandma to the orchard. My mother had followed. They ended up tending the garden while Daddy built arbors and birdhouses and a long wooden table suitable for feasting. I tended myself in much the same way, filling the emptiness created by my mother's recovery with music and friends and a life of my own.

I started taking flute lessons after school with Miss Olivia Meadowbrook, who talked me into joining the cross-country team because a girl needs stamina to play the flute without fainting. At cross-country practice I met Francesca Pordini, who convinced me to run with her at night under the stars while discussing old books and Italy and her brother, Paolo, who loved poetry and ice hockey and playing the saxophone in the jazz band and who somehow ended up dedicating one of his songs to me.

My mother adored the Pordini children. They knew Italian. They weren't afraid of her belief in reincarnation. They called Grandma *Nonna* and taught her new commands: *Nonna, siediti!* "Grandma, sit!"; *Nonna, acchiappa!* "Grandma, catch!"; *Nonna, prendi un bagno, per favore!* "Grandma, please take a bath!" Since Grandma was learning a foreign language, my mother decided to join her. She immersed herself in Italian tapes, subtitled movies, opera CDs. And I would come home from my flute lesson to find the kitchen warm and fragrant, my friends and parents singing along with Figaro from *The*

Barber of Seville, and Grandma waiting patiently to lick the pomodoro sauce from my mother's wooden stirring spoon. "Too much oregano?" my mother would ask her. "No? Just right? Hmm? Oh! More garlic. *Si! Grazie, Nonna! Grazie!*"

She would look up to find me watching her. "Welcome to the madhouse," she'd say happily.

It *was* a madhouse. But it was a glad madhouse.

Even when Grandma got sick. Even when she died and we buried her in the backyard. I played my flute, and we each picked a pear to set on Grandma's grave. We spoke about what she had meant to us. The memories were sweet as ripe berries.

Miss Olivia Meadowbrook said Grandma was a dog with exquisite taste in music. Francesca Pordini called her a fearless running companion. "A good kisser," teased Paolo. Daddy said Grandma was a true retriever, and we both knew what that meant. We had been right in hoping she would fetch my mother and bring her back to us. Uncle Rev, my mother's bachelor brother, thought Grandma might have been an angel. He glanced at Miss Olivia Meadowbrook. "A beautiful, beautiful angel," he said, in a way that made my flute teacher blush. And then it was my turn. "We were playing solitaire and we got stuck," I said. "Grandma was our red seven. She gave us the chance to play out our hand." "True," my mother agreed. "So true. Of course you can only imagine what Grandma meant to me," she added, "she being the reincarnation of my own grandmother."

Miss Olivia Meadowbrook cocked her head and

wedged her brows together, confused. "So, you believe in life after death?"

My mother laughed. My father, too, for all that had led to this moment. "We believe in life *before* death," my mother explained.

"Yes," I whispered. *"Yes."*

A shaft of autumn sunlight illuminated the ancient pear tree. Somewhere in heaven, Grandma wagged her tail.

A Note From the Author

*When I was a special education teacher, I learned
American Sign Language in order to communicate with
my students. Since then, I've studied French, Italian,
Spanish, Norwegian, and Japanese. I'm not at all fluent.
I simply love languages.*

*I believe the language of depression is silence. Whole
families learn to "say nothing, see nothing, feel nothing"
as a way of coping with one member's illness. I think
"Red Seven" is a kind of fairy tale where depression is the
spell cast on the hapless mother. The rest of the family is
affected, as well. (Remember how everyone in the castle falls
asleep after Sleeping Beauty pricks her finger?) In this case,
they spend their lives feeling responsible for the mother's
happiness. When she breaks the silence, she breaks the spell,
and they all appear to live happily ever after.*

I wish it worked that way for everyone.

SHOOFLY PIE

NAOMI SHIHAB NYE

On our way somewhere we sat at this table—
wood clear-varnished, a design to hold the days:
two people talking toward the center,
candlelight on each face . . .
                              —William Stafford

Mattie couldn't believe she dropped the giant honey jar on the floor the moment the boss entered the kitchen after his overseas trip. Have you ever watched a gallon of honey ooze into a slow-motion golden dance around a mound of broken glass?

It might have looked glorious if she hadn't been the one who dropped it.

The boss stared at her with his deep eyes, his mouth wide open. "And you . . . must be . . . ?" he asked.

A secret voice in her head replied, *The idiot. The donkey.* But her real voice said, "The person they hired while you were out of town." Then she said, "I'm so sorry—I'm also very sorry about your father," and knelt down.

You couldn't exactly use a *broom* on honey. A shovel maybe? She had a weird desire to stick both her hands into it.

Or, she might faint. Having never fainted before, she always imagined it as a way to escape a difficult scene. That, or going to the bathroom. "Excuse me," she'd said, many other times in her life. "I'll be right back." At her own mother's funeral recently, she'd spent a lot of time in the bathroom with her forehead pressed against the cool tiles. She felt safe, removed from the grief of what was waiting for her back in the world.

In this case, a huge mess to clean up, and twelve sprouty salads to make, *pronto*. A bouquet of orders hung clipped to the silver line strung over the window between the kitchen and the dining room. She could peek out into the happier part of the restaurant, the eating domain, where regular people with purses and backpacks and boyfriends were waiting for their lunches.

How had she gotten into this?

Long ago, before her mother was diagnosed with cancer, when she still thought she just had migraine headaches, Mattie offered to make dinner by herself. She was twelve. During the whirl of washing lettuce, hulling fresh peas, stirring spaghetti sauce, and lighting the oven to heat the bread, she'd managed to pull down from the wall the giant shelf over the stove that held matchbooks, tea, boxes, spice jars, recipes, birthday candles, half-empty sacks of Arabic coffee, yellowed grocery lists, vitamins, and her mother's favorite cabbage teapot with a china rabbit for a lid. One ear broke off the rabbit and chips of china fell into the spaghetti pot. Her mother came into the kitchen with a wet rag over her head to see what was happening.

Mattie should have known she was destined for disaster.

Today the boss squatted beside her. She felt comfortable to be in the presence of another American-of-Arab-descent, but it didn't seem the right moment to mention it. She'd seen his name on the mail that came in his absence. Despite her clumsiness, he was smiling and mild. "Thank you," he said. "My father was a good man. As for the honey, I think I'll get one of those big scoops we use in the cooler and take care of it myself. Why don't you go back to what you were doing? Don't worry about it!"

She stared after him. What a nice voice! Relieved, she turned back to the counter to sprinkle sunflower seeds and shaved cheese over bowls of lettuce . . . and there was the empty honey bear sitting with its hat off, waiting for her to refill it for the waitress who had shoved it at her—Mattie would suggest the waitresses take care of such details themselves from now on.

Two weeks ago she'd never even thought about being a cook in a restaurant and now she was ready to help run the place.

The boss could have fired her. Some bosses were mean. She'd heard about them from her parents over the years. But suddenly she wanted this job very much. She needed it.

She needed the money, but even more, she needed distraction. It was too hard to be home by herself for the summer since her mother had died the first week of June. Her father was at work all day long until suppertime.

Three days after the funeral, she'd gotten on a bus to ride downtown to the library and, in her distraction, had gotten off too early. She saw the *Good for You Restaurant* staring her in the face.

That's what she needed. Something that was good for her.

So she stepped inside for a late lunch. After ordering an avocado sandwich with cheese, she'd asked the waitress, "Do you like working here?" It was a cozy environment. Large, abstract paintings, mismatched chairs, real flowers in ceramic vases on each table. Ceiling fans, soft jazz playing.

The waitress sighed and shrugged.

Mattie asked, "Do you get to eat for free?"

"Sure. But who needs food? I'm not hungry. You get sick of food when you haul it around all day." She whispered, "Anyway, I'm too in love to think about food."

"With who?" (Mattie wondered why, when someone else whispered, you whispered back.)

"The guy who washes dishes. Augie. If you go to the rest room, you can see him through the doorway. He has long blond hair and an earring."

Who didn't have an earring, these days? Even men who looked like Mattie's father had an earring.

So she walked back to the rest room just to see the love interest of a person she didn't even know, to distract herself from her own thoughts. The dishwasher looked bubbly and clean in his white apron. As if he washed himself between dishes. Slicked up and soapy. He grinned at Mattie when he caught her glance.

"He's cute," Mattie whispered to the waitress, upon

her return. She ordered a bowl of fresh peach cobbler. She'd barely eaten in days.

"The problem with working here right now," the waitress said, "is—we're so shorthanded. Johnny's the main cook, but his grandpa died in Alabama, and he went over to help his grandma out two weeks ago. Plus, our boss Riyad was called to Beirut suddenly for his father's funeral—everyone is dying! Riyad's great, he helps out in the kitchen when he's here. But without them both, it's a nightmare! Riyad thought we needed an extra cook even before everybody left. Do you know anybody who'd like to be a cook?"

Fueled by her cobbler, Mattie was a danger to society. Plus, if everyone was bereaved in this place, she'd fit right in. "I would."

"Do you have experience?"

"Of course!" Who didn't? She'd been inventing sandwiches and slicing elegant strips of celery for years. She made quick stir-frys for her parents and super-French-toast on the weekends. She'd often made her mother's sack lunches as well as her own—her mother had taught at a Montessori school where she had to heat up twenty little orange containers in the microwave at lunchtime every day. None of her students ate peanut butter anymore, she said—they ate curries, casseroles, and tortilla soup.

Mattie even read cookbooks for relaxation some-times. While her mother was dying, she couldn't concentrate very well on novels and found herself fixating on women's magazine recipes describing how to make cakes in the shapes of baby lambs and chicks.

"How do I apply?" The waitress dragged Sergio, temporary cook-in-command, to Mattie's table. He had a frantic glaze in his eyes, but asked a few questions and wrote her phone number down. Then he told her to show up to work the next day. That was it. No application form, no interview. Mattie did not say, "I want to cook here because my mother just died." By the next day she'd applied for a health card, her backpack was stashed under the cash register, and her own white apron was tied around her neck.

Augie, the dishwasher, came out wiping his hands to welcome her.

Examining the menu closely from her new perspective, Mattie tried to memorize it on the spot, while Sergio juggled salad-making with the spreading of mayonnaise on homemade bread. His large hands looked awkward sprinkling wispy curls of carrot among lettuce and arugula leaves in the line-up of bowls.

Looking down onto the top of Mattie's head, he said, "Would you wash those flats of strawberries and mushrooms that just arrived—if we don't get this mushroom soup on for dinner soon . . ." which was how Mattie became his goon.

She wasn't sure "goon" was the right word, but that's what she felt like.

Do this, do that. He never said "please." He gave her the most tedious jobs and quoted Johnny as if Johnny were the god of cuisine.

Sergio didn't know the easiest way to peel raw tomatoes—dunk them into boiling water for three minutes, then pluck them out. That was one of the million little things she'd learned from her mother. Would she be remembering them forever? She could hear her mother's voice steering her among the giant spoons and chopping blocks—a hum of kindness, a *you-can-do-it* familiar tone.

Here in this place her mother had never been, it seemed easier to think about her. Easier than at home where every curtain, dusty corner, and wilting pot plant seemed lonesome right now. The shoes poking out from her mother's side of the bed. The calendar with its blank squares for the last two months. "You know," her mother had said, when there were just a few days left in her life, "this is the last thing in the world I ever wanted to do to you." It was easier right now to be in a madly swirling kitchen her mother had never seen.

"Well, I don't *know* Johnny, okay?" Mattie said to Sergio on the fifth day of heavy labor, after she'd just chopped a line of cucumbers for the daily *gazpacho*. "So he's not such a big deal to me, okay?"

"He will be when he gets back," Sergio said.

He was mixing fresh herb dressings. Mattie had snipped the basil up for him with a shiny shears. She peeled fifty cloves of garlic in a row. Even her bed at home would smell like garlic soon. She'd fallen immediately in love with the giant shiny pans, families of knives, containers of grated cheese and chopped scallions lined up to top the splendid House Vegetarian Chili.

And she liked the view through the kitchen window into the dining room. She started guessing what a customer would order before the order had been turned in.

Every day the same young woman with short dark hair came in, sat alone under a cosmic painting (blue planets spinning in outer space), and ordered a vege-burger and a Healthy Waldorf Salad on the side. She wore dangling earrings made of polished stones and glass. By the end of each meal she was patting her teary cheeks with a napkin.

Was it something she was reading?

Mattie had noticed her as she stood next to Sergio mixing up their Date/Nut/Cream Cheese Delight in a huge bowl. It didn't take many brains to do that. So she could observe their crowd of eaters—bodybuilders, marathon-runners, practitioners of yoga, religion professors, and students.

"Do you know that girl?" She poked Sergio's side so he almost cut himself.

"Watch it! Who?"

"The crying one."

"Huh?"

Men didn't notice anything.

"The beautiful one who comes in here every day, orders exactly the same thing, and starts crying."

He stared disinterestedly through the window. "Actually she does look vaguely familiar."

Mattie speculated, "Maybe she hates our food, but she's obsessive-compulsive and can't go to any other restaurant. Maybe she's in love with Augie, too."

Mattie asked Riyad if she could ring the crying customer out.

"Sure. Do you know how to use the cash register?"

"No."

He showed her. That was the greatest thing about Riyad—he never made anyone feel stupid for not knowing something.

Mattie took the girl's bill and rang it up, whispering, "Is there anything we could do here to make you feel better?"

The girl looked shocked. "Who *are* you?" she asked.

"I'm the person who puts dressing on your salad and makes your sandwich. I've noticed you through the window. Right there—see that little window we have? I started working here a few weeks ago. And you seem—upset. I wondered if you could use—someone to talk to or anything."

The girl looked suspicious. "Do you know Johnny? The cook who runs this place?"

Him again. Mattie said, "He's on a trip. I've never seen his face."

"Just wait," the girl whispered. "It's the most amazing face you'll ever see." She shook her head. "God! He drives me crazy."

"Me, too," Mattie said. She stepped away from behind the cash register so Riyad could ring up someone else.

The girl looked confused "But I thought you said . . ."

"I was just kidding, sorry. I don't know him. Is he your boyfriend?"

"Well, we were dating before he went to help his grandma. But right before he left, he said we were finished—well, he didn't say that *word* exactly, because I don't think he believes in beginnings and endings, but he said—we needed to follow different paths. God, I love him! I guess that's why I've been coming in so often. I'm hoping he'll be back and he will have changed his mind." Her eyes filled up again.

Mattie handed her a Kleenex. "Has he called you since he's been gone? Has he written you at all?"

"Nothing. I've called him maybe four times. His grandma always answers and says Johnny's not there. She must be lying! But you see, Johnny hates to talk on the phone. He doesn't believe in it. It makes him feel—disembodied. So I don't know if he's really not there or if he's simply—sticking to his principles."

"Sorry, but he sounds like a nutcase. How old is he, by the way?"

Her face sobered. "Twenty-one," she said. "But he says he's ageless."

Sergio suddenly stood behind Mattie with a ladle in one hand and a wire whisk in the other. "Are you taking a vacation? Or is this a coffee break I wasn't told about? If you're going to work here, you'll have to carry your weight."

It was his favorite dopey phrase.

Johnny returned the next day.

Sergio was sick and didn't come in.

Riyad had to take his wife and babies to the doctor, too. Even with the *Good for You Restaurant*'s wholesome cuisine bolstering them, they'd all managed to get the flu.

So it was Johnny and Mattie on their own, with one lovesick waitress, another waitress with a sprained ankle, and Augie poking his sudsy head around the corner now and then to see if they needed plates.

Amazing face? Mattie couldn't see it. She thought he had an exaggerated square jaw, like Popeye in a cartoon. Huge muscles under rolled-up white shirtsleeves. Deep, dangerous tan. Hadn't he heard about skin cancer? Explosive brown curls circled his head. He had great hair, yes. He also wore an incredibly tight pair of faded blue jeans. Mattie couldn't imagine he felt very good inside them.

"I'm sorry about your grandpa," she said.

Johnny stared at her hard. "I didn't realize you knew him."

That was mean. No way she would mention her mama when he was as mean as that. She hadn't even told Riyad or Sergio about her mother yet. Immediately Johnny started moving everything around. All the implements and condiments she'd rearranged to make them more available in a rush, all the innovative new placements of towels, tubs, paprika, cinnamon—*whoosh!*—he wanted to put things back exactly where they had been when he left.

And he was muttering. *Rub, rub, rub,* how dare anyone juggle the balance of his precious sphere? "Here!" he roared, lion-like, as he pulled a giant knife out from the lower shelf where Mattie had hidden it, finding it too large to be very useful. "Here is the sword of the goddess! My favorite sweet saber! And what is this pie on the Specials Board that I've never heard of in my life—*Shoofly?* Where did that come from?"

"Well, first from the Amish communities in Pennsylvania. *Americana*, you know? And now, from me." Mattie had suggested the recipe her second week, since it happened to be her personal favorite pie, and they'd sold out of it every day.

"*You?*"

He could make the simplest word sound like an insult. You didn't even want to be "you" anymore. "And who *are* you?"

She brandished her blender cap. "I'm the new—chef."

"Chef? I'm the chef around here. You're the cook, okay? Do you know the difference between the words?"

"I know the difference between lots of words. Between RUDE and NICE, for example." She stalked back to the dishwashing closet.

"Augie, break a plate over his head, will you?"

Augie looked shocked. "Johnny? Johnny's like—the mastermind! He knows—everything! Did you know he even built the tables in this place?"

"I don't care. He doesn't know *me.*"

She served nine pieces of Shoofly Pie that day. Arranging generous slices on yellow dessert plates, Mattie savored the sight of their crumbled toppings over rich and creamy molasses interiors. Her mother used to love this pie.

That day no one ordered buttermilk pie, which apparently had been Johnny's specialty before he went away. His pie was still languishing in its full dish when Mattie wiped the counter at three P.M.

"What's *in* this pie of yours?" he asked her.

"Niceness."

During the lunch rush, Johnny had ordered Mattie around more rudely than Sergio ever did. But now she knew where Sergio learned it. Johnny snapped commands. *"Saute! Stir!"* He kept insisting there were granules of raw sugar on the floor under his feet and making Mattie sweep when he had food all laid out.

"That's very unsanitary, Johnny, to sweep in the presence of food. Didn't your mama ever tell you?" Her words seemed to throw him into a funk.

When his weepy ex-girlfriend materialized, pressing her face up close to the kitchen window for what she hoped might be a welcome-home kiss, he tapped her forehead with his fingertips and busied himself. "Any chance we could spend some time together?" she asked wistfully.

"Sharon, you know what I told you."

Tears welled up in her syrupy eyes.

She said, "Johnny, I think I can make you happy," as he slapped dill sauce around a grilled portabello mushroom on polenta. Ouch.

The waitress and Augie had been found wrapped in a bubbly embrace in the broom closet that morning when Mattie whipped open the door looking for the mop.

Sergio now had a crush on a buff bodybuilder who came in every morning for a peach smoothie, dressed in a leopard-printed tank top. Even the Hell's Angel who appeared only on Saturdays had slipped Mattie a note that said, "Good muffin, baby," drawn inside a heart.

Only Riyad, dear Riyad, seemed able to focus on food and the work right in front of him. One day after work Mattie had told him about her own Syrian heritage and her mom's death coinciding with his dad's. Did she only imagine it, or did tears well up in his eyes, too?

After that they both threw Arabic words into their

talk. *"Yallah!"* Speed it up. *"Khallas!"* Enough already.

Some days Riyad refilled the bins of flour and apricots and sunflower seeds in the grocery section with careful attention. Some days he polished the front window glass till it glittered. Lots of bosses might never lift a finger. One day Mattie found him down on his knees on a prayer rug in the cooler chanting in Arabic. She respected his devotion to service. He told her he had dreamed of owning a restaurant ever since he was a little boy who loved to eat, wandering the streets of Beirut. Only the ten-year war had made him leave his country. Mattie admitted she had trouble with Johnny's attitude. Riyad whispered, "Listen to this: When he first came to work here, he was our baker, not our chef. He asked me, 'Do I get paid while the bread's rising?'"

"Have you been in the service or what?" Mattie asked Johnny, on her forty-fourth day at work. It was truly summer now, each day swelled full of ninety-eight-degree heat. Midsummer in Texas, people forget what a cool breeze ever felt like.

"Why do you ask?"

"You act like a general. I think you'd like me to salute you."

"Well, you're full of it, too."

He was furious that she had started revising the soup list. Today she was making a spicy peanut stew from Eritrea with green beans and sweet potatoes.

"Where is Eritrea?'" he asked her. "And what makes you think our customers will know of it if I don't?"

"East Africa. The whole world is tired of your black

bean soup, Commander. It's time to BRANCH OUT."

Johnny always stared at her as if he needed an interpreter.

Riyad went wild when he smelled that peanut stew cooking. "I want some! When will it be done?"

Mattie told Johnny the customers were also tired of his boring bouquet of alfalfa sprouts on top of his little salads, too. "Let's try lentil sprouts for a change. Or nasturtiums. Come on." Basically she was weary of watering them. She wanted to witness some different curls of life in the sprouting jars under the counters. Anyhow, an East Indian professor on the other side of town had just gotten *e-coli* that was traced to alfalfa sprouts, and she felt nervous about them.

An anonymous food critic from the newspaper had eaten at the restaurant recently and written a glowing review. "Happy to say the *Good for You* menu offers new sparkle and a delectable, mysterious dessert called Shoofly Pie. Not to be missed." Mattie made three extras that day and they all sold out. A lady bought a whole one for her book club.

On the tenth of August, Johnny asked Mattie to sit down after work for a cup of mint tea with him.

"You think you're really clever, don't you?" he said, tapping his spoon on his cup.

"Not at all," she said, startled. "I certainly don't. In fact, I usually think I'm pretty dumb. It's just that you were used to making all the decisions around here and it's been really hard for you to share them. I don't know why. I certainly wouldn't want to make all the decisions."

"You wouldn't?"

"No way. I think sharing them is better."

"You do, do you?"

He was staring at the top of her head as if she had two small horns erupting.

Then he said, "Would you like to go to a movie with me?" and she almost fell over backwards out of her chair. Late afternoon sunlight hung suspended in the air. She could smell the warm sweetness of molasses from the pies just out of the oven.

"Um—I'm sorry—I can't. It's not a good idea to mix business—and pleasure." She really wasn't much of a dater—now and then she went out with friends in groups, like migrating monarch butterflies, or ducks— but she simply could not imagine going around with this troublesome—chef.

He looked thunderstruck. "Are you serious?"

"Very."

He shrugged. "It was a good movie, too."

"Which one?"

"I'll never tell." Then he hissed, "What—do you just stick around home with your mama after work and learn new recipes?"

Tears rose up in Mattie's eyes. He stared at her.

"My mother," she said, "died right before I started working here. For your information."

"Why didn't you tell me?"

"You weren't here. Plus, when you got back, you weren't very friendly."

One thing about loss—you decided whom to share it with. You could go around day after day and never give anyone a clue about what had been taken from you. You could hold it inside, a precious nugget of pain. Or you could say it out loud. When you trusted enough. When you felt like it.

"I didn't feel like it."

You could place it on the table.

Johnny spoke softly now. "I'm sorry. But didn't you know I'd just been at my grandpa's funeral myself?"

"Yes."

"And he was like a daddy to me? He raised me when my own daddy took off? And my mama was already gone?"

Now tears shone in Johnny's eyes. It was a restaurant where every single person ended up crying at one time or another. "Well, I didn't know that," Mattie said. "That must have been really—hard."

She found herself with her hand on his arm.

"I'm sorry, too," she said. "I know you really loved your grandpa a lot."

He looked up sharply. "You do? How do you know that?"

"Trust me."

So many times during the days he'd mention little things his grandpa used to tell him. How to sharpen a knife. How to "swab the decks"—what Johnny called cleaning a counter.

Now he said, "Let me tell you about my grandpa's favorite corn bread," and described it so deliciously, with real pieces of fresh corn tucked into it, that Mattie had the idea they should concoct a meal based on beautiful things his grandpa used to cook for him when he was growing up. Greens, corn bread, quick-fried okra, sweet potato casserole, vinegar coleslaw, pecan pie, and, since their restaurant didn't serve meat, a special vegeburger seasoned with sage, his grandpa's favorite spice. They could do it In Memorium (privately), but on the board they'd just call it "From Johnny's Grandpa's Special Recipes."

They could even put white daisies on every table because those were his grandpa's favorite flowers.

The menu was so popular, they kept it up there three whole days. As customers were paying, they said, "Johnny, tell your grandpa we loved his food." No one told them he was dead.

Then Mattie said, "Okay, Riyad, what did YOUR daddy eat? Your turn."

For three days they served lentil soup, *baba-ghanouj*, okra with rice, and falafel sandwiches.

They played Arabic music in the restaurant.

Riyad seemed deeply emotional about it. He placed his father's dashing young photograph on the register. He gave Johnny and Mattie raises.

Sergio had left them by that time. He'd gone to sell boring used cars over on San Pedro, because he could make three times as much money over there. "But it won't taste as good," Mattie told him. They'd hired a grandmother, Lucy, to take his place. Lucy loved their new recipes as well as their old ones. She said, "Did you know the name 'Shoofly' came about because the Amish people would shoo away the flies that came to land on their cooling pies when they took them out of the oven?"

Johnny said, "We don't have any flies in here. Mattie catches them in her fists the minute she sees them."

Then they did Mattie's mother's recipes. Mattie had a very hard time deciding which ones to do. Her mother had been a great cook, once upon a time, way back in that other world where things were still normal.

The menu board featured a special green salad with oranges and pecans, fragrant vegetable cous-cous with raisins, buttermilk biscuits, and of course, Shoofly Pie for dessert. "I think your mother had a sweet tooth," Riyad said, staring dreamily at the full plates lined up on the counter.

"That she did," said Mattie, swallowing hard. Her mother had had everything: the best singing voice, the kindest heart, the kookiest wardrobe—she never felt shy about combining checks and stripes and wild colors.

Mattie brought in a tape of her mother's favorite blues singer, Lonnie Johnson, to play while they served her food. Mattie's father came over from his office to eat with them.

"This is kind of like that Anne Tyler book, *Dinner at the Homesick Restaurant*," he said. Mattie sat with him. He put his hand over her hand. "What a rough summer, baby."

Mattie said, "It's also like our own private Days of the Dead." On November 2, people in south Texas made shrines to their beloved deceased family members or friends, arranging offerings of their favorite foods among the lit candles and incense.

"So who's homesick for Shoofly Pie?" asked a diner seated at the next table. "It's great!"

"Everybody," Mattie said. "Everybody who never lived a simple life." In some ways, you could choose what you remembered and what you did with it. Memories you chose to treasure would never fly away. They were like an adhesive stuck to the underside of your heart. Maybe they kept your heart in your body.

Riyad had an idea that they could offer their In Memorium menus to the general public, too—letting people bring in groups of recipes belonging to someone they had loved who was gone now, and the *Good for You* staff would revise the recipes to become healthier, then serve special meals designated "Camille's Favorite Ratatouille Feast" or "Jim's Special Birthday Dinner" . . . what a thought.

"Is it creepy?" Johnny wondered out loud. "Will people feel like they eat here, then they die?"

"No," Mattie and Riyad said at once. "It's comforting. TRUST US."

"How do you think an omelette looks better, folded over, or simply flipped? Should we slice the small strawberries in the fruit bowls or leave them whole?" Suddenly Johnny was so full of questions, Mattie could barely answer them all. He seemed to have softened somehow, like beans left to soak.

Sometimes when Mattie came in to work, she'd stop for a moment inside the door of the restaurant as if she were frozen. She'd stare all around the room—the tables, the chairs, the paintings, the vege-salt shakers—trying to remember how the place had looked to her before she'd known it from the inside out.

Now she had the recipes memorized, the arrangements of provisions on silver shelves inside the cooler, the little tubs the blueberries lived in. Even in her dreams she could hear the steady *clip-clip* of their best silver knife against the cutting board.

One day she told Johnny she admired his speed when he had ten things to do at once. He grinned at her so he *almost* looked handsome. He said, "Do you ever think how we'll all remember different things when we're old? When this restaurant feels like a far-away shadowy den we once inhabited together—I might remember the glint of the soup tureen in the afternoon light or the scent of comino, and you might remember—the gleam of my ravishing hair?"

"You wish." But she liked him now. She had to admit it. She really liked him.

One day Riyad said, "Everything is changing!" He gave Mattie a poem by Rumi that read, "The mountains are trembling. Their map and compass are the lines in your palm." The first cold norther had swept down from the skies and everyone was wearing sweaters.

That was the day she resigned. She had too much work to do at school now to keep on working here. Plus, she was feeling steadier. The restaurant had been Good for Her in all the ways it needed to be, and she could move on. She could cook better dinners for her father at home, with all her new experience. She could have dinner parties for his friends.

It shocked her how Johnny responded to the news of her departure. He shook his head and said, "No, no, no, baby," as if she were a little dog at his feet.

"What do you mean, no no no? Yes yes yes! I have homework piling up on me. I have a major paper to do that I haven't even started! My dad and I haven't even cleaned our house since my mom died. I'll miss this place terribly, but hey, I'll still come in and eat! And maybe you'll go to another movie someday and let me tag along, what do you say?"

Johnny stared at her. He'd been making Shoofly Pie on his own lately—good thing, because everyone still ordered it. Riyad and his wife presented Mattie with a mixed bunch of happy-looking flowers and a card: "This is your home now, too!!! We love and appreciate you— free lunch any time!" Johnny kissed her, first time ever, on the top of her right ear. Her mother used to kiss her there.

A Note From the Author

When I was in college in San Antonio, I worked as a cook
in a wonderful, wacky natural foods restaurant called
The Greenwood Grocery, owned by a couple of kindhearted
musicians, Sarmad and Sharda Brody. I think we were
paid a dollar an hour in those days. It seemed like a
lot of money to me. The restaurant is long gone now, but I
still miss it when I pass the building on my own street
where it used to be. I've always remembered the swirl of
characters, flavors, and fragrances that filled our days there
and have made different attempts over the years to write
about it. While this story is fiction, the setting is the way I
remember it.

YOU'RE NOT A WINNER UNLESS YOUR PICTURE'S IN THE PAPER

AVI

The way I heard it, Billy always wanted to have a bike good enough to be a winner at the Staltonburg Memorial Day Bicycle Race. As it turned out, the day Billy celebrated his twelfth birthday, he got just what he wanted.

Now there wasn't a lot of money in the Kinley household—Betty Kinley being a single mother. So the birthday bike wasn't exactly new, having been purchased second- (maybe third-) hand from Hank Schuster's New and Used Bike Shop out on Vine Street.

Didn't matter to Billy. In his eyes that bike was something right out of a dream. Love at first sight. The moment he saw it he just knew it was going to be the winner of the big Memorial Day race.

Winning was mighty important to Billy. His father had been a stock car racer, of sorts. Billy didn't know too much more about him—the guy took off when the boy was two—but he knew *that* fact. Tacked to the wall in Billy's small room was a faded five-by-five newspaper picture of his father holding up a trophy he'd won. So it was true.

Of course, the marriage business wasn't anything Betty—Billy's mother—spoke about much. "Something happened," she'd say. That's pretty much all Billy knew, and there was kind of an understanding between mother and son that he wouldn't ask.

That morning Billy had slept in on account of it being both his birthday and a Saturday. So his mother gave him the bike when he was still a tad sleepy.

When the boy came into the kitchen of their mobile home—the home wasn't going anywhere but sat in the middle of the Thirty-third Ave. Trailer Park and Laundromat—his mother kissed him and gave him a big hug—as if his birthday had moved her son into some kind of manhood.

Billy enjoyed the attention. He was an only child, but no one ever tires of being well loved. And Billy's mother loved him a lot. She worked extra hours as a secretary at the Invincible Insurance Company plus weekend clerk at the local Piggly Wiggly supermarket. She was trying hard to save money for the real house she so much wanted for the two of them. Many a time they talked about what color the kitchen curtains were going to be in that house his mother was saving for. It was a bit of a joke with them. She wanted blue curtains. He wanted red. If you would have asked Billy what Heaven was, he probably would have described a house with red curtains. In any case, Billy spent a fair amount of time without her being around.

Billy's mother had hidden the bike under a sheet.

When she led him to it, she covered his eyes with her hands. Crying "Happy Birthday," she lifted her hands, then flicked away the sheet.

Hank Schuster's New and Used Bike Shop had done a fine old job of refurbishing the bike: new tires, new seat, new handle grips. The color—a splendid fire-engine red—was spiffed up so that the nicks and scratches that were there seemed quite minor, hardly worthy of notice. And maybe Hank did a little something extra. Folks knew something of Billy's family.

"Is it mine?" Billy asked, hardly believing what he was seeing. His mother did not—could not—go in for big gifts very often. This was—and he knew it—a big gift.

"It's your twelfth birthday," Billy's mother said, and gave him another hug.

"It's just what I wanted," Billy said, still in a daze. "It'll win that race for sure."

"Yours to be responsible for, have fun with," Betty added, proud to have made her son so happy.

A worried look came over Billy's face. "But . . . wasn't it very expensive?" he asked. He knew how hard his mother worked, always scrimping and saving, how they were nibbling on the edge of being poor.

"Billy, it's your twelfth birthday," his mother reassured him.

"I know, but . . ."

"Tell you what," she said, guessing he needed some justification for his joy, "your job isn't just to enter the Memorial Day Bike Race, you got to win it."

Billy nodded in happy excitement. "First-place prize for kids my age is twenty-five bucks."

"Great," she said. "When you win it you can put it into the house account at the bank."

"I could?"

"I'm counting on it," she said with a smile that suggested that was absolutely part of the deal.

"I'll do it," Billy promised. "And if I win, they'll put my picture in the paper. Maybe Dad will see it."

Though Billy sometimes said things like that, his mother never commented. Not on that subject.

The boy rushed his breakfast, yanked on his clothing, and hauled his new bike outside. It was a beautiful spring day. Sun shining. A touch of balmy breeze. You couldn't buy a better day for a new bike.

Billy insisted his mother watch the first ride. Thrilled, he straddled the bike, pushed back on the brakes, bounced the seat, touched his fingers to the frame. He was so enraptured that when he finally pushed off, he did wobble a bit, enough to add a little more excitement to the moment. After a couple of seconds, though, he got himself right, found his bike legs, and rocketed off, racing around the lot. The yard-wide grin on his face was all the thanks his mother needed.

But Billy being Billy, he said, "Ma, it's perfect. The best bike in the whole world. A winner. I love it. Thank you *so* much."

That whole morning Billy rode his bike around the trailer park, showing it off to friends and any other kid he could. Grown-ups, too, for that matter. "It's going to win the race, don't you think?" he said to everyone. Everyone agreed it was a fantastic bike. No one mentioned the nicks and scratches. They wouldn't. People liked Billy Kinley.

By around noon, when Billy finally got back home—

his mother had gone off to her Saturday clerking job—he found a rag beneath the sink and worked the morning's dirt off the bike. He didn't just rub the frame down and scour the fenders, he cleaned each and every spoke.

That afternoon, after he made himself lunch, he went out with his best chum, Joey. He and Joey went beyond the trailer park, out by the old meadow, and raced about all afternoon.

Billy loved going fast, standing up on the pedals, swishing the bike from side to side as his legs pumped like locomotive drivers. He really wanted to be a racer. Like his dad. He rarely said anything about that because it gave his mother a look of pain.

That afternoon he had wonderful fun. He didn't win every race—Joey won some— but he won often enough to give him real hope that when the Memorial Day Bike Race came he would win it all. The bike was going to do great things for him.

That night he dragged the bike into his bedroom. It barely fit. He thanked his mother again, and went to sleep one very happy kid.

All the following week, soon as the bus dropped him home after school, he hauled out his bike—he insisted upon keeping it in his room—and raced around.

Next Saturday he registered for the Memorial Day Bike Race. When he did, he received a numbered Coca-Cola–sponsored bib. "D-87." It made him feel even more excited. He and Joey practiced hard, too, hour after hour, out in the field. It didn't take long before Billy was winning almost every time. And let me tell you something, Joey wasn't a bad biker.

That Saturday night—it was two weeks before the big race—Billy asked his ma for permission to bike to school.

Betty wasn't so sure.

"It's only three miles," Billy assured her. "It'll be part of my training for the race."

"Three miles?"

"Charley"—Charley Coolidge, a pal of Billy's—"told me that. And guess what? He goes a back route that doesn't have much traffic."

"It won't get stolen at school, will it?" his ma asked.

"Lots of kids bike to school," Billy assured her, not really answering her question.

There was some talk about getting a lock, but that was forgotten. Billy hadn't seen locks on other kids' bikes. He didn't want to seem like a sissy. Besides, he didn't want to put his mother to any further expense.

To be sure about the safety, Billy's mother drove the route Charley Coolidge had suggested. It clocked out exactly at three miles and seemed safe enough. She granted permission.

That Sunday afternoon Billy cleaned his bike up again. I'll tell you, it positively glistened. He even asked for and received from a neighbor a dab of car wax for the frame and chrome handlebars. As he cleaned, he realized he'd already come to know its few scratches. He told his mom they were part of his bike's personality. "Nobody's perfect," he told her with a shy smile and a look to some far-off place. "And you have to learn to forgive."

His mother smiled her sad smile, but didn't say anything.

It was a proud Billy who rode his bike to school and

back on Monday and Tuesday. While in class he left it with the other bikes behind the school, near the two bike racks the school had provided. The racks were not sufficient for all the bikes, so lots of them were just dumped on the ground. Billy wouldn't do that to his bike. He leaned it carefully against a tree. The tree being in leaf, it shaded the bike from a too-hot sun.

On Wednesday, right after three o'clock dismissal, when Billy came to collect his bike, it was gone.

At first Billy thought he had just forgotten where he had left it, and went searching. But as more and more kids claimed their bikes and took off, it became obvious that his bike wasn't just gone, it had been *stolen*.

As Billy began to realize what had happened, shock set in. With tears in his eyes, and a whole lot of pain in his chest, he kept roaming the school grounds, over and over again, searching. Maybe, he kept telling himself, someone had taken it by mistake, or had only borrowed it. Maybe they would bring it back.

The point is, he didn't find it.

Finding it hard to breathe, Billy went into the school office and reported what had happened. The school secretary gave Billy a whole lot of sympathy, even as she said such things happened a lot.

Then she said, "I can't believe one of our kids took it. Did you have a lock on it?"

Billy had to admit that he did not.

Then the secretary said, "Billy, why don't you go over to the police station down on Fifteenth Street and report it. Stolen bikes get dumped. Joyriding, I guess. So they find lots of bikes."

Trying to be hopeful, Billy ran over to Fifteenth Street. He had been inside the police station once, the time his pal Joey's ma filed an accident report, a fender bender.

The police station was small, a one-level building, with heavy glass doors. Bullet proof, kids said. Inside, it was a dreary place, one long room with a low ceiling. A couple of tables stuck out from one wall. Some faded posters hung about to remind people about safety at railway crossings and kids leaving school.

At the end of the room was a counter, behind which a policeman sat talking on the phone. He had a weather-beaten face, a cowboy mustache, and eyes that suggested he had seen too much.

When the policeman hung up the phone, he glanced up and said, "Hey, kid, how you doing? What can I do for you?"

Billy got his chin over the counter and spoke right up. "My bike got stolen."

"Oh-oh. When did this happen?"

"Today."

"Hey, I'm sorry. Where did you see it last?"

"At school."

"Had it been locked up?"

"No, sir," Billy said, small voiced.

"What's your name, son?"

"Billy Kinley."

"Tell you what, Billy Kinley," the policeman said, "I'll give you a form that you can fill out. You know, describe the bike. Do you know what kind it was?"

"It was a Mercury. Red. I was going to race it in the

Memorial Day Race. It's a great bike. A winner. Like my dad is. I got it for my birthday."

"Well, maybe your dad can help fill out the form. Did the bike have an identification number on it?"

"I don't think so."

The policeman pulled a long face. "Hate to tell you, Billy, but it's hard to prove a bike stolen without that ID number. Come on over here. Let me show you something."

He led Billy out of the building to a fenced-in area, a cage-like place. Some thirty bikes were stuffed in there.

"These are bikes we picked up," the policeman explained. "You know, stolen or lost. You're welcome to look, but if yours just got taken, it's not likely there. Not yet. You might come along tomorrow and check. And bring that form. But, like I said, without an ID number, it's going to be hard to claim or prove any bike is yours."

That evening Billy told his ma what had happened. She was as upset as he was.

Billy said, "I went to the police and they gave me a form. He said my dad could help fill it in."

His mother considered her son wearily. "Suppose I could do it, don't you think?"

"Yeah."

"Hey, let's go hop in the car first. Maybe we can spot it around town."

Billy and his mother cruised the neighborhood, going by Billy's school, driving in and out of streets. For an hour and a half they searched but saw nothing of the bike. It was only darkness that made them quit.

"I'll tell you one thing," Billy said with a sigh.

"What's that?" his mother asked.

"Just because we can't see it," Billy said, "doesn't mean it's not somewhere. Has to be."

When they got home Betty helped Billy fill out the police form. "Wish we knew the number of the bike," she said.

"It didn't have one," Billy said. "But, Ma, I know all its nicks and scratches. I'd know it for certain if I saw it."

Next day, right after school, Billy brought the filled-in form to the police station.

The same police officer took it. "You're welcome to check out back again."

Billy did, but his bike wasn't among the recovered ones.

Now, with the Memorial Day Race coming up fast, Billy wasn't ready to give up.

Over the next few days, soon as school let out, he trotted right on over to the police station to see if his bike had been found. Went so often, the desk officer came to know Billy pretty well. But the bike did not show up.

Staltonburg, the town Billy lived in, wasn't exactly big. Searching for the bike, he could wander over a lot of town. Each day, though he couldn't go everywhere, he covered a fair bit of territory before heading back home. He liked to be there when his mother got back from work.

It was on Friday—just a few days before the big race—when Billy found his bike. He was on Alameda Street when a boy, an older boy, went whipping by. In a flash, Billy recognized his bike. He had not the slightest doubt. "Hey!" he yelled.

When the kid on the bike didn't stop, Billy ran after him, calling, "Stop! Stop!"

Finally, the kid on the bike halted.

Billy, almost out of breath, caught up with him. He was someone Billy had never seen before.

"What do you want?" the kid demanded. He was a teenager, a tall, skinny boy, with an acne-pocked face that put the moon's surface to shame. He wore his sideburns long and kept the peach fuzz under his nose. His black hair was slicked back. He wore tight jeans, and a white T-shirt with a pack of cigarettes rolled up in one sleeve. On his left arm was a tattoo, an American eagle.

"What do you want?" the teenager said to Billy.

Billy was eyeing the bike, checking out the nicks and scratches he knew so well, making sure it was his. No doubt about it. It was. He said, "That's my bike."

The teenager grimaced and said, "Says who?"

"It's mine," Billy insisted. "You stole it from my school."

The teenager dumped a whole river of cuss words over Billy.

Billy stood there, taking it in without a blink. But when the teenager was done, Billy said again, "You stole it."

"Prove it," the kid said.

"Got a V-shaped scratch on the inside of the rear fender," Billy shot back. "Go on, dare you to look. Double dare you."

Now it was the teenager who said, "It's mine."

"Give it back," Billy said, and put his hand on the handlebar. The kid knocked the hand off.

"It was my birthday present," Billy shouted, all red-faced. "I was going to be in the Memorial Day Race. It's a winner. Give it back!"

"It ain't yours, and *I'm* going to be in the race," the older kid said, shifting the bike away. He also lifted his leg, prepared to take off.

"I'll call the police," Billy screamed while balling up his fists. "Give it back!"

The teenager slammed his foot hard down on the pedal, so that the bike took off. The next moment he was wheeling away, fast.

Billy raced after him. "Thief! Thief!" he yelled. He got to the end of the block, took the turn that the kid had taken, but the kid had gone. Disappeared.

Boiling with fury, Billy searched one street after another. But the thief and bike were gone.

Billy tried desperately to think what to do. Knowing his ma wouldn't be home yet, he raced to the police station. When he got there, he had to wait in line. First there was a couple who were engaged in a heated argument. Then there was an old man reporting that his Social Security check was missing.

When Billy finally got up to the desk, it was the same desk officer he had spoken to before.

"Hi, Billy. Got some news?" the policeman asked.

"Some kid on Alameda Street has it."

"Good for you!" The policeman reached for a pad and pencil. "What's the kid name?"

"Don't know."

"Where's he live?"

"Don't know that either."

The policeman put down his pencil. "Hey, Billy, I thought you said you found it."

Billy said, "The kid who stole it was on the street. Riding it. I told him to give it back, but he just cussed me out and took off."

"Where'd he go?"

"I don't know."

The officer sighed and leaned over the counter, elbows down, hands clasped, and spoke kindly. "Billy, there's not much we can do about it, is there, if we don't know who took it, or where it is."

"But the race is in three days!" Billy protested.

"Don't I know it. Hey, I'll be the finish-line judge. Look, I'll put a call in. Can you describe the kid who had it?"

Billy did the best he could. It wasn't much. He mentioned the cigarettes in the white T-shirt. The sideburns. The tattoo.

"Where was the tattoo?"

"On his left arm. An American eagle."

"That's something," the policeman said. "We'll try." He didn't sound very hopeful.

"I've got to get it back," Billy said, retreating.

The police officer turned to the police call box and in a loud voice began to alert the town's three squad cars.

When Billy got home, his mother was there. Full of rage, he told his tale. Betty was indignant, too. "Come on," she said. "Get in the car. We'll go look."

Billy and his mother did search, cruising about the areas where Billy had last seen the teenager with his bike. But either the kid was lying low, or it wasn't his neighborhood. They caught no sight of the boy or the bike.

"Maybe you scared him," Billy's mother said as they drove home. "Maybe you scared him so much, he dumped the bike and the cops will pick it up."

Billy stared out the window. "I got to get it to win," he said.

Come Saturday and Sunday—Memorial Day weekend—Billy spent all of his time roaming Staltonburg. He checked in with the police station three times. By this time, the desk officer greeted him like an old friend. But Billy's bike wasn't in the cage.

"Hey, kid," the policeman called to him as Billy, his face long and sad, walked by after checking the bike cage yet again. "Come here."

Billy obliged.

"Look here, son. I don't think your bike is going to show up. And I know you want to be in the race tomorrow, right?"

Billy nodded.

The officer lowered his voice. "Now what I'm suggesting," he said, "isn't exactly dotting the i's and crossing the t's. But you *could* go into the bike cage, find yourself a bike. Then you *could* tell me it's the one you lost, and I *could* sign it over to you. After a few months, when no one claims them, we sell 'em anyway."

Billy didn't say anything.

"I mean," the policeman continued, "even if you didn't want to do that, you could, see, just *borrow* it, and then bring it back after the race. Am I making myself clear?"

Billy shook his head. "I can only race my bike," he said. "It's the winner," he said.

"Okay, kid," the officer said. "Just trying to help."

"Thank you," Billy said.

Memorial Day was one glorious day. The sky was deep blue with a few fluffy clouds moving along like lazy old lambs. The sun was warm and mellow. Trees were fresh with new spring green. Lilacs were in bloom, too, along with some lilies and quite a few roses.

The Staltonburg Memorial Day Parade took place along Market Street. It formed up at the corner of Rochester and Elm at ten A.M. sharp. In the lead was the Boy Scout honor guard, two Eagle Scouts who carried the national and state flags. They were flanked by two Boy Scouts and two Girl Scouts, each carrying dummy white rifles. There were Cub Scouts and Brownie out-riders, beating out a marching rhythm on small snare drums. The drums were held over their stomachs with red, white, and blue sashes.

Behind them came an old Packard convertible. A 1939 model, spiffy white and bright.

Sitting next to the driver was the mayor. He was waving to the crowd. In the backseat was a highly decorated World War II veteran.

After the lead car came other vets, the Foreign Legion, the Veterans of Foreign Wars, in their uniforms. The reservists marched behind.

Once the military passed, the police and volunteer fire departments in their cars and trucks went by, their sirens wailing and lights flashing. Caused some dogs to howl. Then came the clubs, the 4-H, the Down Homers. After that came the Ladies Town Welcoming Committee, the Friends of the Library, and other groups. They were all there, the people who owned and ran the town, strutting by, waving to friends and family who were lined up two and three deep along the sidewalk.

At the tag end of the parade came the kids on their bikes. They ranged from toddlers on tricycles and tiny two-wheelers with training wheels, helped along by their parents, on up to the older boys. These guys were wearing their Coca-Cola–numbered bibs.

Billy Kinley—with his racing bib on—was watching from the sidewalk along with his mother. They were looking for his bike.

He and his mother had worked out a plan of action. Billy had remembered the teenager saying he intended to be in the race. If Billy saw the teenager or his bike, he would tell her. Parade or no parade, she would wade right in and do what she had to do to get the bike back.

But Billy didn't see his bike. Once, twice, he thought he did. He even called, "Ma!" But those were false alarms. The parade went by without any incident. Or Billy's bike.

"Maybe," Billy's mother suggested, "you scared him off so he won't be in the parade."

All Billy said was, "That bike's a winner."

"Come on. Let's see the races," his mother suggested.

The police and fire departments ran the races in the five-and-dime parking lot. The store being closed for the holiday, some portable bleachers had been set up. The race course had been marked off with some wooden orange crates.

Billy and his mother found some seats in the stands, up high, so they could observe everything that went on.

"If you see him," Billy's mother reminded her son, "just point him out. No fighting."

To the far right a starting line had been painted in red. A policeman with a starting pistol stood by.

The finish line, at the other end of the lot, had another painted line, blue. The finish judge—just as he said he'd be—was Billy's friend, the policeman.

There was a card table set up in front of the bleachers with a bunch of trophies lined up. They were for the winners. With each trophy was an envelope with twenty-five dollars.

A reporter—with a camera—from the local paper, the *Staltonburg Defender*, was there, too. His assignment was to take pictures of the winners.

There were also a microphone and speaker by the fire chief's hand. He called out which race was to be run.

First up were the toddlers, on their tricycles. Just as many girls as boys. There were lots of murmurs and laughter. Words like "cute" and "adorable" could be heard. It was fun, but nothing serious. In fact, when the starting gun went off some of the toddlers were so scared, they just sat there and cried—which brought laughter. But the rest were off, pumping knees like little robots until one red-faced little guy crossed the finish line.

Billy watched it all intently, scanning the crowd of bicyclists and bikes. Not that he saw what he was looking for.

The races went on, one after the other, gradually working their way up the age ladder. After each race the finish line got adjusted so the course became longer.

When it got to the twelve-year-old level—Billy's race—he stood up, straining for some sign, any sign, of his bike. His mother stood with him, a hand on his shoulder.

They didn't see a thing.

Some other kid—Billy had never heard of him—won. His pal Joey came in second. Billy slumped a bit, but insisted on standing, watching. He was still hoping he'd at least get his bike back.

Next came the teenage-level race. There were a whole lot of kids, all jumbled up around the starting line. It was pretty much all boys now, though a couple of girls joined in.

"If he's coming, he should be down there," Billy heard his mother say. Billy had thought as much himself.

The policeman lifted his pistol and fired.

At first the racers were bunched up, so it was hard to see who was in the lead. Bit by bit, though, as the leaders formed, the pack began to get strung out.

"There it is!" Billy screamed and pointed.

His mother looked. Sure enough, in the lead was this tall kid pumping away like crazy on a red bike that was much too small for him. He was fast, too. The bike was winning.

"That's him. That's my bike!" Billy kept screaming. "It's winning!" He scrambled down from the stands. His mother was right behind him, trying to keep up, saying, "Excuse me, please. Sorry," as she worked her way through.

By the time they got down to the ground Billy saw his red bike zip across the finish line. The kid riding it lifted both arms high over his head as if he had scored a touchdown.

Billy raced after him.

The teenager had spun the bike around and was facing in. Billy's friend, the police officer, was at the finish line. He was moving toward the winner, hand extended for congratulations. But that's also when the policeman noticed Billy charging across the lot. The teenager must have seen him, too. He spun the bike around and took off, double time. If he moved fast when he was racing, I'll tell you, it was nothing to what he was doing to get away from there.

Billy kept running after him, trying to catch the thief.

He could not. Within seconds the teenager was gone. With the bike.

The policeman, who had seen the whole thing, sized up the situation right away. "Was that your bike?" he asked. "Was that him?"

"Yes," Billy gasped.

The policeman took a step in the direction the thief had taken, but saw how futile it was and stopped. "He's gone," he said.

"But my bike . . ."

"It's gone too, Billy." Maybe it was the look on Billy's face that did something to the policeman. He suddenly said, "Follow me."

He started walking back along the course. Billy followed, as did his mother, who had caught up.

The policeman reached the trophy table. He beckoned Billy over. "We got some kind of a problem here," he said to the fire chief, who was sitting behind the table. "The winner of that last race was riding a stolen bike. The bike belongs to this kid. I can vouch for that."

The fire chief looked at Billy. Then at the policeman. "What am I supposed to do?" he asked.

"The bike won, didn't it?" Billy's friend said. "You should give the trophy to this boy."

Billy spoke right up. "I don't want it," he said.

"But, hey, kid, your bike won," the policeman said. "So you won." He looked at Billy's mother, trying to get her to do something.

Betty Kinley just stood there.

"I lost," Billy said, and ran off.

The cop snatched up the trophy. "Are you his mom?" he asked.

Betty nodded.

He offered her the trophy. After a moment, she took it.

Back at the mobile home at the Thirty-third Ave. Trailer Park and Laundromat, Betty found Billy on his bed, hands behind his head, staring up at the ceiling.

"You won the trophy," his mother said, holding it up.

"The bike was the winner," Billy said. "Not me. You're not a winner unless your picture is in the paper. Dad'll never find me." With that said, he rolled over so his back was to his mother and the trophy.

Betty Kinley stood there, gazing down at her boy. After a moment she sat down on the bed, by his side, stroked his hair, and said, "Billy, you've convinced me. The kitchen curtains can be red."

A Note From the Author

"Loss," my dictionary tells me, appears to have evolved from an old English word meaning "destruction." I find that an interesting notion because nowadays I think the way we use the word suggests something more along the lines of a "something missing." And if you miss something, the natural tendency is to keep looking for it, trying to replace that which is gone.

Yet all things change. It was an ancient Greek philosopher who once said, "You can't step into the same river twice." This awareness of constant change is a singular human perception. But change, inevitably, means loss. Which means all people suffer loss in big and small ways. Yet people deal with loss differently, too, sometimes with a shrug—and forgetfulness—sometimes with constant yearning and a continual search for replacement.

The way we deal with loss—change—is perhaps one of the truly defining elements of our personalities. Too often the modern world pretends it does not, should not happen. And maybe that's the greatest loss of all.

SEASON'S END

WALTER DEAN MYERS

Summer had ended with a rich and sudden fury, and now the chill of autumn brought its deep shadow across the neatly kept infield. James "Jimmy" Sims was tired. His knees ached, and the weight of the bat seemed ponderous as they approached the last games of the season. He knew the fatigue wouldn't help things with Miriam. He had called his wife twice during the one-week western swing, once after the Seattle game and again after the game with the Angels. They had made small talk, had strung words together in careful order, and had hung up knowing that things were still wrong between them.

Now they were in the League Championship Series and they were behind, two games to one, and he knew that someone would call it a "must" game and some-one else would attempt to analyze why they hadn't won the game before and that they would get it all wrong. The only reason, his first manager used to say, that the other team wins is because when the game is over they have more runs.

"Hey, Jimmy, got a minute?" A sportswriter, fulfilling his own caricature—cigar, light leather jacket, the tape recorder in a suede bag slung over his shoulder. The same questions again.

"Sure."

"How come Day didn't put in a pinch hitter for Brown yesterday? Brown has only got one hit off left-handed pitching in the damned play-offs!"

"I don't know, Mike. Just one of those things. You guess right and you're a hero."

"You know what I think?" The writer chewed on the cigar, spat out some tobacco, then pointed with it. "I think he's scared of Brown after that blowup in the locker room. That's what I think."

"I don't think anybody's scared of anybody."

"Then how come he didn't pinch-hit for him?"

Jim looked away and shrugged. Why the hell did anybody ever pinch-hit for anybody?

"Can I ask you one more question?"

"Sure, go ahead."

"You've already said you're hanging up your glove, so I know this series means more to you than any other series you've ever played in." The writer took him by the arm and assumed a tone of confidentiality.

"But with all the crap that's been going on with this ball club, don't you feel like gagging? You want to go out a winner, and all these guys want to do is get a little more glory for themselves, that's all. Am I right? Am I right?"

"I guess," Jimmy said, knowing he'd have to wait until

the next day to see what the sportswriter was going to say in his column. No matter what had actually been said, the story was already filed away in the guy's head. Jimmy looked around; the stands were almost filled. Hoag was calling for the infielders and he jogged out toward second base. Hoag took balls from a coach and started banging them around the infield.

The ball went to Dempsey at third and he hotdogged it as usual, gunning it to first. Then it went to Hernandez and then it came to him. For a second he had thought about hotdogging it, just to show Dempsey that he still could, and then he realized that he had already scooped it up two-handed, the way he had done for fifteen years now, and was throwing the ball smoothly to first. He usually never thought about fielding, throwing, or even hitting a baseball. He had tried to explain it to Miriam once, that thinking about what they were doing was how ballplayers got old, that a good ballplayer existed only in the fragile matrices of imagination and space and nowhere else. That somehow, in his mind, there was a vision of himself doing all those things that needed to be done. The white misshapen blur of a ball streaks across the green infield, and long before he could ever think of moving legs and feet, or shifting weight, there would be the memory of a dream that knew where the ball must go and where the glove must go and how first base would look as he turned, already throwing, to beat the man pumping furiously to the base. Only after a thousand balls hurled against the garage door, a thousand imagined plays to which only he and God and his father's old Camaro had borne witness, was any of it even possible.

Somewhere along the way there was a fusion of mind and body that edged on greatness. A fusion that could stop a ball hit sharply into the hole and that could make a ball leap from the bat into places where others could only watch and lunge hopelessly as it disappeared into seas of colored shirts and plastic beer cups.

Game time. The players were introduced and "The Star Spangled Banner" sung by someone who had forgotten it was the national anthem. His team took the field. Jimmy watched from the shadow of the dugout. His muscles twitched along with those of the fielders ringing the immaculate infield. Perhaps a half beat behind. Perhaps a quarter beat.

He didn't like sitting on the bench. He felt helpless. Still, he wanted the team to win. That would always be there. The first six innings flew by with the score tied one to one. There was a tension on the bench, a feeling that the other team would suddenly break out and score a lot of runs. In one corner of the dugout a cameraman kneeled, daring anyone to be interesting. Some of the players assumed attitudes that they felt would look good on television.

Bottom of the sixth. Two away. Gaiters doubled down the left field line. Dempsey, up next, asked the umpire to check the ball. He'd been in the league a year. The manager looked at the pitching coach and then away. Dempsey watched the first ball go low and away for a ball. The second ball was over the center of the plate, and Dempsey took it for a strike. A third pitch was belt high on the outside corner, and Dempsey watched it go by as the umpire signaled the second strike.

"Flash that bastard the sign again!" The manager's neck was red. A thousand lines made orderly crisscross patterns down the back of it.

"What the hell's he up there posing for?"

The next pitch was inside, and Dempsey swung, sending the ball trickling toward third base. Dempsey hesitated, weighed by the gravity of the moment. Then, realizing that the ball would not be foul, he began to run. The first base coach waved his arms frantically as the ball narrowly beat Dempsey to first.

"Where's his glove? Where's his glove?" Someone handed the manager Dempsey's glove and he dropped it on the floor of the dugout near his foot. Dempsey, already on the field, waited for someone to bring the glove out. He kicked at the ground to show that he was angry with himself. Hernandez patted him of the behind as he went by and told him that his glove was still in the dugout.

Dempsey came into the dugout, looked for his glove, and saw it at the manager's feet. He walked toward it, fumbling nervously with his sunglasses. Jim looked away as the manager kicked the glove across the dugout toward the water cooler. Dempsey had another year in the league, at best.

In the eighth the score was still tied, but in the top of the ninth the other team scored twice. The first two men up in the bottom of the ninth grounded out, and Jim was called to pinch-hit.

The crowd was still there. They were the home fans and were hoping for something to happen. Jimmy stood at the plate, swinging the bat, establishing his rhythm.

He looked at the stocky pitcher, glove against his left thigh, hat pulled down over his eyes. He would want a strikeout to end the game. The first pitch was slightly outside, and the umpire called it a strike. The second ball was a high curve that had gotten away from the pitcher, and Jim slapped it into right field. He watched it as it dropped in front of the fielder. The crowd cheered as he rounded first, glanced at the right fielder cocking to throw the ball, and retreated back to the bag. Golden was up next. He swung at the first pitch and popped it up. It went high over the infield, and Jim ran to second and around it as the short-stop pounded his glove. A second later the game was over.

"You think you'll take the next game?" Another sportswriter talking to an outfielder in the locker room. *How to say that the ball was round? How to say that it was thrown and caught and batted and that, yes, the sun would surely rise?* He heard the answer. Yes, they would take the next game.

The best year was the year that Cowens, the owner, had moved the training camp from Florida to Arizona. Jim had hit .312 and was second in the league in total bases. He also played on the all-star team that year and had made close to $23,000 in royalties for having his name on a baseball bat, the Jimmy Sims signature model. He had even been on a game show where they had given him jokes to rehearse and he had memorized them and even practiced them in front of a mirror the day before only to find out that the laughter, even though the show was taped in front of a live audience, was canned. The black housewife who was supposed to be his partner on the show didn't make it in time, and they had to recruit a black secretary from their advertising department. Miriam had laughed when he told her about it.

"Jimmy Boy,"—the manager said his name as if the "boy" were part of it—"You're starting tomorrow."

"That's good," Miriam said later. "He tell you why?"

Why? Jimmy shrugged. Because Day felt that they were going to lose, that was why. It was a gesture. He would take Dempsey's place at third. The kid would be blamed for the series if they lost. Day would say that the turning point was when the kid didn't hustle to first base. It was the key word, *hustle*. The kind of word that didn't have a lot of meaning until someone in power applied it negatively to your name. The kid didn't hustle. He goofed off. It was something that sports fans thought they understood. Everybody on a team was a hustler if the team won. If they lost, somebody had to be goofing off.

"Are you still sure about quitting?" she asked.

"I'm sure," he said. "It's been okay, but . . ." he was going to say that he was still a young man. Only thirty-six. He had given baseball fifteen of those years.

"Can we go away someplace after these games are over?" she asked.

"You're that sure we're going to lose this series?"

"I meant . . ." Her hand fluttered nervously in front of her face. "Whenever it's over."

He looked at her, and she was looking away from him. It was coming on with a rush. They had talked about divorce in neat, correct phrases as if they were not holding their breath between words. *"We've lost something . . ."* she had said. What had they lost? A step down the first base line? A microsecond of bat speed? What had they lost?

"Please," she added. The word seemed to wrench itself from her bosom.

"Sure," he replied.

He felt weak without knowing what strength he was lacking. He knew of the distance between them that he could not somehow manipulate, and of feelings begging to be shaped into purpose, but where was the strength to come from. It was not a new feeling for him, this weakness. He remembered a time in Boston when he had been called on to pinch-hit. It had been the third time that week, and he had struck out once and hit a weak grounder the other time. He had stood at the plate and hoped for a hit. He had looked at the pitcher, and somehow, whatever it was that the pitcher was, it was more than Jimmy had brought to the plate. He had felt the weakness in his arms as he fouled off the first pitch. The next pitch was out of the strike zone, but he had swung anyway, lofting a short fly that fell in left field and had pushed in the winning run. It had been that day, standing at the plate and hoping for a hit, pleading with his heart for something that his wrists and hands would have once demanded, that he had decided to give up baseball.

He had not wanted just to give up, to surrender it, head bowed, to bodies tempered in the heat of more recent summers. He had wanted to end at a time of impeccable logic, to walk away from the game laughing at its foolishness, amused to have participated. But somewhere, somehow, the moment had passed.

But it was what he had had to offer her, the game, and

his mastery of it. The game and the constant dream that went with it. Jimmy had been baseball for so many years, he had been the game. That was what he had brought to her. Where in his soul, now that the game was ending, would he find more to offer her?

"You going to get a hit tomorrow?" Her voice broke through, startling him.

"Sure, why not?"

"Get a double," she said, standing. "Want a beer or anything?"

"Fine." He thought about the house in Brentwood, about how he could fix up the basement. He had always said that he would never put his trophies up, but now he thought about it. He had gone to a sportscaster's house once; the guy had been a great infielder on a championship team. They had drunk rum and cokes while Miriam had talked to the sportscaster's fat wife.

Eventually he had been dragged downstairs to what was called the trophy room. The trophies were all shined and polished, their rounded surfaces distorting the faces that stared into them. There should, he thought, have been ashes in the cups.

The next game day was overcast, and there was a slight wind blowing in from left field. The first four innings went easily enough. Ground balls and short flies added up to zeros for both sides. In the fifth inning the bases were loaded when Jimmy came to the plate and he walked, bringing in a run, and the next man singled, bringing in two more. The inning ended with him on third and his team three runs ahead. There was an air of expectation as they took the field in the sixth, properly accompanied by pounding gloves and throwing the ball around the infield after each out. The seventh inning was the same.

The ninth inning. The first two opposing players walked, and Day brought in Bell to close out the game. The next man singled up the middle, a ball that just as easily could have been a double play had it gone a few inches to either side of its perfect path. The score was three to one, and Jimmy reminded himself that the next batter liked to swing on the first pitch.

They played for the double play and got it as a second run scored. It was three to two, and the bases were empty again. Bell threw four straight balls, and Day signaled for a new pitcher as the batter trotted to first. The on deck guy, a thin kid from the Dominican Republic, watched the new pitcher warm up, then stepped in and hit his second home run of the series. They were behind four to three. The next batter hit a ball just inside the third base line. Jimmy lunged to his right, felt the ball's impact in his glove, scrambled to his feet, and threw to first. The umpire's thumb jerked violently into the air. The batter was out.

He was up second in the home ninth. There was a man on first, no outs. The third-base coach called him over and told him that they were going to put on the hit-and-run sign but to ignore it.

"I think they're stealing our signals," the coach said.

No, Jimmy thought, they were just playing better ball.

Jimmy swung at the first pitch and missed. He wiped the sweat from his palms onto the front of his uniform. There was a knot in his groin, a hardness that he had often felt before. He stepped back into the batter's box and watched the second pitch sail high and outside. He stepped out of the box again and hit his cleats with the small end of the bat. Rituals. Magic rituals that would somehow ward off losing. He rolled his shoulders forward and back. There was a game at risk, or was it a world? An image of Miriam flickered through his mind as the umpire spoke to him. He twisted his hands around the bat as he stepped into the batter's box. On the mound the moon-faced insolence of the pitcher was shadowed by the angled visor of his cap.

There was a quick move toward first. The runner dove back in. The umpire jerked his fist into the air. He was out. Jimmy stepped out of the batter's box in disbelief. How could anyone get picked off in the bottom of the ninth when you were trailing? One out. The kid trotted toward the dugout, his eyes glazed over. Jimmy knew he would go to his grave dreaming about his mistake.

The next pitch was belt high and away, and he swung. The sound was right, and even before he had lifted his head the ball was past the first baseman's straining arm and headed for the right field corner. Jimmy ran, head down, no need to look until he reached first. The coach was pointing toward second, and Jimmy made the turn. The base was never so distant. He never moved so slowly across the brown dirt of the infield. He saw the second baseman set himself for the throw and realized that he might be thrown out. He dove, head first, past the bag to the left and reached back with his right hand. The second baseman, thinking he had misjudged his position, spun toward Jimmy's body and over the straining arm. Safe. The noise of the crowd was a low and distant buzz. The umpire asked him if he wanted time to dust off his uniform. Yes, he did.

He stood on the base as the pitcher took the ball. A step off the bag. Watch the pitcher. Watch the catcher. Watch the short-stop nervously edging toward the plate. For a delicious moment the game was caught in the frame of the lengthening autumn sun. For a moment it was all there again. The jerky motion of the pitcher. The swing. The crack of the bat and the ball skidding toward the third baseman. Jimmy moved quickly back to second as the ball flew across the infield. They were down to one out for the season.

The young pitcher leaned forward, the ball turning in his bare hand behind his back as he looked for the catcher's sign. Jimmy kicked the bag and took a step off, and another one. The pitcher went into his stretch, held it as he looked back at Jimmy, then threw the ball. The impact of the ball against the bat was sharp, and Jimmy broke for third. Ahead of him their short-stop was leaping high into the air to intercept the rising line drive. The season was over.

Jimmy showered and dressed quickly, stepping gingerly past the crew of technicians reclaiming the television cables that would have been used if his team had won. He promised everyone that he would be at the party the next day and shook hands with the equipment manager who was flying to California that night. He knew many of the others wouldn't be at the party, but it was easier pretending that there would always be a tomorrow.

"You gonna write me out in Utah?" Cooley, a relief pitcher, asked.

"You learn to read yet?"

"No, but I'll work at it if you're gonna write."

They exchanged friendly punches. Reassuring man-to-man stuff. Jimmy started to say something else, something meant to be funny, but felt the tears stinging in his eyes. In the tunnel leading to the exit ramp he passed a sportswriter rushing to the other dressing room. How to say that the ball was round?

Miriam was in the car when he reached it. "I'm sorry," she said.

"It's okay. We were lucky to get this far."

"Where to?" She started the engine.

"Anywhere. No, let's drive to Brentwood again. Maybe we can take another look at the place we were thinking of buying. I don't know, it's late."

She drove along until they reached the Long Island Expressway and then the Southern State. "Do you remember the exit?" she asked.

"It's . . ." He looked out the window. Nothing looked familiar. "I don't know where we are."

Miriam took the Hempstead exit, slowing as they went through the city streets.

"Thanks for the double." She broke the silence, her voice a jig jag of emotion. "Somehow I thought you did it for me. Isn't that silly?"

He thought back on the game and remembered that he had, indeed, doubled. He looked at Miriam and saw that she was crying, spilling out her secrets in the dark confines of the car. He suggested that they stop for a bite to eat and he went in and got coffee and ham-burgers.

"A kid recognized me in the diner," he said. "He asked me if I felt bad about losing the game."

"What did you tell him?" She had pulled herself together.

"I told him that I felt bad," he said.

"I wanted you to win, too," she said. "I thought when you were on base you guys were going to do it."

"Well, I . . ." He started to speak and stopped as a sudden swell of emotion came over him. He turned and smiled at Miriam. "I don't want to learn to be a good loser," he whispered.

"Neither do I," she said, putting her hand on his.

He listened as she went on, missing most of the passion-muffled words, understanding her eyes. He thought of more to say, more about being alone without baseball, and stumbled awkwardly through them as they drove.

She listened to his words without answering, glad for hearing them, taking her eyes from the highway now and again to look at him, to see that the words were coming from the right place.

On the way home she meandered almost aimlessly through the small Long Island towns, only vaguely in the direction of the city. He began to unwind, slowly. He noticed that his hip was hurting from where he had slid into second. Later she would ask him about the game, and he, more tired than he had ever thought possible, would tell her as much of it as he could remember.

A Note From the Author

In my early thirties I still considered myself a fairly decent basketball player. But one day, on the court down on Sixth Avenue known as "The Cage," I found myself grabbing a player's jersey as he went by me. There had been a time I could have given the guy a half step and still stopped his shot. I had enough experience in the game to know what he was going to do, but my feet responded a split second later than they should have. That split second put me on the sidelines with a soft drink as a new team took to the court. I realized it was not the first time I had "grabbed" at a passing jersey. If there was indeed such a thing as a coming-of-age moment, that had to be the opposite of it. It was a moment I'll never forget.

THE RIALTO

JACQUELINE WOODSON
AND CHRIS LYNCH

In that movie, *One Flew Over the Cuckoo's Nest,* Jack Nicholson plays this guy who gets sent to jail for statutory rape. But then he acts all crazy and belligerent in jail, so they send him to this psych ward. He does all kinds of wild stuff there, like stealing all of the patients in the psych ward and taking them fishing and bringing in ladies and booze. Stuff like that. The first time me and Ivan went out, he took me to this movie house that showed that movie and right when the women showed up with the booze Ivan grabbed my hand. At first I just thought, *Okay, so this is a weird scene for him to be grabbing my hand.* But then it kind of struck me how sweaty his hand was and I knew he'd spent the whole first hour of that movie trying to figure the best moment to reach over and clutch my fingers. That's what he was doing— clutching my fingers. Not even touching my palm or rubbing it like guys who know what they're doing.

· · ·

"There goes Ivan's car again," my little sister says.

"Don't touch that curtain."

"'S not gonna make him disappear. He's crazy. I *told* you he was crazy."

"Shut up."

My little sister moves away from the window and leans back against the wall. Her breasts are starting to grow and the rest of her body's starting to curve out around them. *She has smoky eyes*, Ivan said the day he met her. *Both of you have those smoky eyes.* After that, Delia's eyes looked different to me. All of her looked different to me. And now, all these months later, with her body catching up to those eyes, I feel scared for her. I don't want her to grow into me. I don't want her to ever want something real bad.

"Why are you wearing that stupid shirt?"

Delia looks down. The shirt is tight and has GIRL written in white letters right between her two tiny breasts.

"You *gave* me this shirt. *You* used to wear it. What are you talking about?"

"It's a dumb shirt. I should have thrown it away."

That day at the movies, Ivan had his hand wrapped around four of my fingers and my thumb was just hanging out, like it wasn't part of my hand. I let him hold those fingers though and you know what? I didn't feel anything. I stared down through the blue movie screen light at our hands—his all pale and mine all dark—and I tried to feel *something*. Some kind of miracle of us together in that south end theater with couples all around us being white on white and black on black. But I didn't. Then Ivan reached over with his other hand and just sort of rubbed my palm with two of his fingers. It wasn't in a player way—like the way guys learn how to touch girls in certain places and make them all crazy. It was more in an—I don't know. Months later I would learn that it was in an Ivan way—but that afternoon in the theater it just felt right and whole and good. Soft. Like the most important thing in the world to Ivan was the palm of my hand.

My mother tells me I spend my life in two places— looking to the future—all scared of it—and looking in the past—all filled up with regret. *You never stay in the right now, Caryn*, she says. And now I know why. Because the right now sucks. The right now is this thing inside of me and me too scared to really figure it out. The right now is Ivan cruising by in that stupid car like he doesn't even notice this neighborhood is white-free. The right now is me not even being able to keep water and crackers in my stomach some days and being more scared of the pain of getting rid of this thing than the pain of keeping it. And there's a part of me that's praying that it'll just kill itself right off—all those stupid Ivan-Caryn cells stop multiplying and dividing and doing all their freaky biological math on my body and just . . . just stop.

———————•———————

"That's right," Caryn said as we watched the closing credits of one more old film we had only half-watched.

"What? What's right?"

"That sense is better than nonsense."

"Ah. That. Did I say that? Okay, but truth be told, Caryn, doesn't nonsense feel better?"

She sighed, which was always good. A sigh, a pause, any small thing that indicated a tremor in her unshakable certainty was a good thing. It brought us closer together. Made her more like me. Flawed.

I couldn't see her though, in the total dark, in the wake of the film. We would do that, stay in the old movie theater all slunk down and blended into the seats like we were embedded in the upholstery, long after the show ended. It was a thrill to us, at least as important as the film itself.

"Sorry, Iv. I'm constitutionally incapable of agreeing with that. Nonsense isn't better than sense. It just isn't. Can't be."

But she was holding my hand, which is a whole different animal from me holding hers. It was absolute darkness in the musty theater and it was all ours and damn comfortable way down there in the plush velvet and alone. As Caryn talked and held my hand, we were no longer simply us. We had exceeded us and were voices hanging there, weaving in and out of each other, twining and splitting and rejoining again. But for Caryn's warmed voice on the back of my hand, I'd have lost any contact with the physical reality of us at all. My body wasn't my body, it was a sound. Caryn's voice wasn't a sound, it was essence.

"It's important to be sensible, rational, in this world, Ivan. You know that."

"I believe sense is overrated."

We let it go there. That was in the days when we knew what to do. When we knew how to proceed and how not to. We simply found each other in the dark, shut up, and leaned into each other.

That was the Rialto. Beautiful old theater that showed old movies. We let ourselves out a little later, making sure nothing was disturbed and the door was locked tightly behind us. We didn't want to ruin a good thing.

The Rialto is closed now.

———————•———————

I remember when I hear Mama's feet on the stairs. The Merwin poem from a long time ago. I remember first the subway in New York City—how loud it and everything else was. I was twelve. The week before I had started bleeding and it felt like it does now—everything was muted and sad and weird—but without the vomiting. I remember my father at the kitchen table the evening Mama told him about the bleeding—how he looked at me like I was somebody, no, not somebody, some*thing* strange and far away. Not far away like weird, but more ethereal—like I had risen up onto some pedestal that he had to bow down in front of. It was all there—in his eyes when Mama said, *Caryn became a woman this morning*, and all I wanted to do was slide underneath the table and disappear taking all those stupid pads and Mama's pride and Daddy's fear along with me. Just zoom, be out of there. Gone. Instead of walking into the life trap. Because even then I was heading straight for it. And a week later as the four of us sat on the subway heading uptown, I looked up and saw the poem.

> *Your absence has gone through me*
> *Like thread through a needle*
> *Everything I do is stitched with its color.*
> —*W. S. Merwin*

And I read the words over and over again, imagining the color of absence, wondering if Merwin was male or female, sad or happy when the poem was written. And later on, I found out Merwin was a guy and it was strange to think a guy could write those words about somebody. I didn't think much about guys when I was twelve. That first day I bled, Mama explained again about the baby-making thing, about love and my body being a temple. And that night when Daddy came home and looked at me that way, I imagined him praying in front of it, his head bowed, his arms out in front of him the way the Muslims bow toward Mecca. And I tried to wrap my mind around the idea of a baby inside of me but it seemed too ridiculous, too far away in some stupid grown-up world to have anything to do with me.

"Why are you sitting in the dark?"

I jerk up off the couch and blink when Mama turns the lights on. The room is bright, too bright, and she, still in her work suit and heels, is too big and bright in it. I take a deep breath and feel my heart move against my chest.

"What's wrong with you, Caryn? You look like you saw the devil."

I sit back on the couch and close my eyes. "I don't feel good."

Mama comes over and puts her hand on my head. "You're burning up, girl." Her hand feels cool against my forehead. *Don't ever move your hand, Mama. If you do, I'll break into a thousand pieces and blow away.*

I start crying then, hard and silent. All the weeks and Daddy's eyes and Mama's hand and the poem are inside of me trying to get out. And the stupid baby. It's a baby. A baby.

"Caryn," Mama whispers. "It's okay, sweetie. It's okay."

Mama sits down beside me and I lean against her shoulder. She smells sweaty—and tired, if tired can be a smell, and I breathe her all in, taking hard deep gulps between sobs.

"What's wrong, sweetie?"

"I was thinking about Daddy," I say. A half-lie. My father has been dead for two years now. When people ask, I tell them how it happened—early in the morning on a sunny day with no one expecting it. Yes we were shocked. Yes we cried. Yes it was years ago but the place he filled up in our lives is still empty and open.

"Talk to me, Caryn."

But I can't talk and after a while, Mama stops asking and we sit there, me crying hard and loud and Mama whispering that it's going to be all right.

———————•———————

I'm going to keep coming. I have to.

There are lots of reasons. She might think she doesn't want to see me, but I think maybe she doesn't know what she wants. Or maybe she knows what she wants but she doesn't know what's best. Or she thinks I don't know her, but maybe I do. Or maybe she thinks she knows me but she's got it all wrong.

Those all sound like perfectly viable reasons to me.

The truth is, I'm going to keep coming because I don't know what else to do. Every day I don't see Caryn we slip just that little bit further away. We cannot slip any further away. It is an awful place, away. It is an unthinkable place.

So every chance I get, I get into the Charger, and I drive it over to Caryn's. Uninvited, yes. Unwise, possibly. Unwelcome?

I can't believe that.

The flutter of curtain up at that window where she carries on her vigil is a sign. She doesn't want it like this, I don't want it like this, and still we are like this. But when it snaps, when we wake up from the nightmare part into the beauty and realization part, I want to be here at her fingertips. It is what I can do for her, no matter how hard she makes it for me to do it. It's all been hard, me and Caryn, every bit of the way. And it's all made sense after a while.

So here I go, up the block, and down again. Swirling round and round and round her until it makes nothing but sense to both of us.

———•———

This morning I saw a crocus almost open and it sent me home in tears. Last night Mama made rice and hash and I thought if I didn't get away from the table I'd fall into my plate and dissolve into a puddle of vomit and not-baby and used-to-be-Caryn.

But an hour ago, I started thinking about that movie. And, all crazy, mixed up with it was the first time I ran my fingers through Ivan's hair and how different it felt from mine. How all I wanted to do was spend the afternoon with my fingers moving through his hair again and again and him looking at me in that way he has that's all full of wanting to know every single thought I ever had. Every single thing about me.

An hour ago, I started thinking hard about desire. And how I wish I had never been born. And how I hope this baby never wishes that. And I can't stand still or move or eat or cry or scream. I am stuck in this stupid right now with Ivan's lips that I hate breaking into a smile in my head and his palm on my face then on my neck and then on and on until the beginning of us and the stupid black and white of us and the stupid, stupid boy and girl of us is dissolved into this *baby*. It's a *baby*. It makes me sick and it grows and grows.

"What did you love about that movie?" Ivan asked me that day. We were on the street, our hands in our pockets, walking far apart from each other like the school friends we were most of the time.

"What makes you think I loved anything about it?"

Ivan smiled, that smile that from that day on would remind me of Jack Nicholson—with his black ski cap pulled down over his arched eyebrows and only one side of his mouth lifted.

"It was all right," I said, moving a little more away from Ivan.

He sniffed under his arm. "What?"

"Nothing. I just need some air."

"But we're outside, C."

"I know. You're like a cat, though. The way they suck infants' breath right out of their lungs."

Ivan looked over his shoulder. "What infant?"

"I don't know."

And I didn't. Not yet. Not then. Because that day, there was nothing to know. Sometimes I think we live just walking right into the life trap that's set for us. Me and Ivan hadn't even kissed yet and we were walking, fast and all confident. Just sort of flirting and pulling away, then flirting some more.

Ugh.

And right there—almost a year ahead of us—there it was . . . is. Just grinning and beckoning. Saying, *Keep coming, y'all. Just keep on coming.*

———————•———————

On the fourth circuit of my fourteenth visit to the neighborhood that doesn't want to know me, I finally get a little lucky.

Caryn's sister, Delia, steps out the front door.

I jerk the wheel, pull the Charger to the curb, and abandon it. I am walking toward the house while Delia stands and takes a long, weary look around.

"Hey," I say, stepping a little quicker as she walks off the stoop.

She looks back over her shoulder. "Oh, no. Uh-uh." She picks up speed.

I'm stunned at first. She looks so much like Caryn like this. From behind anyway. Maybe it's the pursuit thing, the feeling that I was always chasing after Caryn, and still am really, and so I got to know the back of her as well as I did the front and so here we are again in all too familiar territory.

But I'll take it. She is looking like Caryn, even if Caryn never thought so. And my heart skips a flurry of beats over it.

"Come on, wait up, Delia. I just want to talk to you for a second."

"One! There you go. Your second's come and gone. Bye."

"Please?"

"What's it, my turn? You gonna stalk me now? I'll call a cop. Or better yet, I won't."

Delia lets out a small laugh, and for the first time I become aware of appearances. I need to be more aware of appearances. Appearances matter. I'm chasing. I'm chasing Delia. I'm chasing Delia down Delia's street. I'm the only white guy using this street now, may well be the only one to use it all day, and I am using it to chase down one of its residents.

What I'm doing is not advisable.

What else is new.

"I wasn't stalking anybody."

She knows this. I know she knows this. Delia is a bright girl. A knowing girl. I know she knows the real deal, because she was a witness. As much as anyone was, she was a witness. She shook her head and wagged her finger and clicked her tongue and *tut-tut-tutted* at me every time she got a load of how I was with Caryn, but it was wonderment much more than it ever was disapproval.

"Okay, you're not a stalker. So don't start now. I got nothing to say to you."

As if to underscore the point, she accelerates just slightly, not so that she's running, not as if she has any fear of me, but just as a way of saying she wants no part of this.

I have no choice but to go faster myself.

"How is she?" I ask, breathless, though I've barely begun to run.

"Sick. That's how. Leave Caryn alone."

Christ, Caryn. I stop right there, turn, and look up toward her window. I am, at this moment, as humiliated as I have been yet, and that is after no shortage of small and large humiliations through this whole thing. What is she thinking as she's watching me chase her little sister? Is she thinking oh my god what has it come to? Or is she thinking, because she is finally seeing, that she can't be doing this to me anymore? I am half-glad I look like I do right now, because we are only talking about the visuals, and too right she should have to see. Because the truth is, I have been feeling just like this, desperate, for some time now.

So if it's sympathy I'll take it. If it is pity, bring it on. If it is appreciation for the length and breadth of my big-hearted stupidity, yes, ma'am, here I am.

And if it is disgust and exasperation, and the final conviction that I am just proving to her what a great stupid waste of her precious time I am, not to mention a polluting of her fine gene pool, then I am ready, finally, to play out the scene here on the sidewalk. Because this can't go on.

The window is open, but the lace curtain's still drawn. I can't see her, and more than anything at this moment, I want to. My heart throbs, like it's been punctured and is now pumping blood helter-skelter through all parts of my chest cavity. I keep angling, to try to steal a vision.

"Hey," Delia calls from a block away.

I turn just as she ducks into the first storefront she passes.

By the time I get there, she is standing, holding the door. Then she lets go. The door closes in my face. I push my way in.

"How long were you going to stand there, Romeo?" Delia asks as she approaches the counter. She is squinting at the shelves behind the woman behind the counter. There are canned goods and lollipops and batteries and Slim Jims. Delia pauses in her shopping to look at me.

I finally answer. "Until Juliet came to the balcony, I guess."

"Dreamer," she says calmly. "Crazy boy."

She goes back to browsing. There is also a coffee-maker and a tray of doughnuts with a Plexiglas dome over it. There is a Slush Puppie machine with the fake cup on top that whirls around and around to say, yo, we got Slush Puppies in here, in case you didn't know it. But the cup isn't spinning at the moment. There are three circular tables near the front window of the little shop, under the backward-stenciled lettering, BREAKFAST.

"Come on," I say. "Talk to me."

"No. Don't want to be seen talking to you, I just wanted to get you away from my house. Caryn's gonna chew off both of my ears as it is . . ."

"Who's going to see you? The place just opened. There's nobody anywhere yet. Let me buy you a coffee."

"Coffee makes your teeth brown. Lady, you sell singles?"

The lady, who I think has not had her own badly needed first cup yet, just shakes her head.

Delia turns to me. "Okay, nuts-boy. You can't buy me coffee, but you can buy me smokes. Then I'll give you ten minutes."

"Great." This, to me, is just that—great. I am so close, one degree of separation away . . . I can smell her, can breathe Caryn essence off Delia. "But you have to stop calling me nuts and crazy and stuff. Deal?"

"Nope."

"Okay, deal."

I get the cigarettes, and a lemonade for myself, and the two of us take seats one table away from the window. The street outside is nice and quiet, just like the shop itself.

"Where are you headed to anyway?" I ask. "You have a job?"

"No. Just like to be up and out of there early these days. Gettin' kind of close quarters in that apartment about now. You got nine minutes left."

I take a long drink, and watch as Delia takes a shallow drag off her cigarette. She smokes the way a lot of young girls seem to do it, as a fashion. The smoke barely seems to reach her lungs before she is expelling it again, sculpting a wispy blue bauble of a cloud and watching it rise with some satisfaction. Then, quickly, she does it again, refining technique. Half a minute later there is a stagnant, hazy thin wall between us and I am thinking it again, the resemblance is a lot stronger than Caryn thinks it is, or at least says it is. It's as if she is afraid that her little sister is going to be as burdened by beauty as she is, so she just denies it entirely. She believes that, Caryn does, that she can bend the world, make things true and untrue, with the force of her mind. Sometimes I believe she can.

Sometimes not.

I have this urge to tell Delia everything. Which, fair enough, is one insane urge. I would only prove her right, and finish myself off in the process, if I didn't check myself. She was leery of me at the best of times, and now she makes little show of having sympathy for me at all. But there she sits, cool and hard, strong and smart and Caryn-like only with the pivotal un-Caryn-like advantage of being with me.

"Six to go," Delia says.

The urge. To tell her how it happened, which, for whatever million interlocking reasons I have not told completely to anybody. To describe how, once I had had the sensation of being aligned, laid out, pressed up against the length of Caryn, toe to hip to shoulder to lip, I have been completely unable to feel anything else. That's what I keep aching to do. To make it make sense. To make the bad parts melt away and make the ungodly good parts make sense to somebody else. So that somebody, somebody who is part of Caryn, say, looks across a table and says, well then sir, you may indeed be crazy, but you may also just be entitled to it.

And then possibly help me. To make right be right again.

"I want to see her, Delia. Do you think maybe . . ."

"I do not think maybe."

I pause. Not to plot strategy, since I haven't got one, but out of plain naked need. "Help me out," I say.

Delia's eyes go wide as she looks out the window. "You're a pretty hard guy to get a message to. Listen, serious. Go away. And stay away. You're only going to run into some trouble, creeping around this neighborhood all hours. Nobody wants to see *you*, but nobody wants to see *that* either. Right?"

"Well," I say, scrambling for the bright side. "Then I'll just earn tragic-romantic-hero-in-the-gutter points."

Delia's just as good at the downside.

"No, you'll just earn bashed-up-ugly-white-guy-in-the-gutter points. Which won't help you any."

Delia stands.

I remain seated, trying to elongate the moment.

"Time's up," she says. "I have to go."

I feel the rush, the voiding, as it all gets away from me, again. "I only want to have a chance . . . to be, like, with her, with *this*." I have my hands out, cupping the tiny invisible something in them. "To do right."

It's as if she doesn't realize I have finished. Her questioning stare. Like that could not honestly have been what I wanted to say. Like I *had* to have a better accounting of myself than that.

"So why'd you go and ruin her life, then?"

She shrugs at me, like, nothing personal, just fact.

I don't say anything. I nod. She waves the cigarette pack at me. "Thanks," she says.

"Thanks," I say.

The door slaps shut and Delia is shaking her head at me as she passes the plate-glass window with BREAKFAST stenciled on it, backward to me, rightways to her.

---•---

My mother doesn't cry when I tell her. She looks away from me and nods, slowly as if the words are sinking past her skin and blood and bones and finally finding a home in her marrow. Her head moves like that, fluid, up and down, again and again.

"You can't have it here," she says.

"I know."

"The neighbors will make you miserable. You don't want that."

"I know."

"What do you want?"

And I start bawling then because she doesn't say why or how could you or you're killing me, Caryn. No. She just nods and asks what I want. But there is so much more behind her nod. A sadness. Slipping around those words floating through her marrow. "I don't know, Ma . . . I think I want to keep it but I don't want to keep it. I don't know . . ."

I am standing against the window. Even without looking, I know his car is moving down my block. Again and again. Circling. Like some hungry-ass vulture.

"I want to go away, Ma." As the words leave me, they become truer. I want to be far away from Ivan, from everything that ever meant Ivan. And when this baby comes maybe I'll love it or maybe I'll pass it on to someone who can. I don't know but I don't want any of this right-here-right-now stuff anymore.

Mama rises and wipes her hands on her jeans. She comes over to where I'm standing and presses them against my face. Warm and soft. I will miss her hands. And Delia's smoky breath and eyes. I'll miss the three of us as we were yesterday and the day before and a year before that.

"I'm sick to death of Boston," I say, meaning I'm sick of Ivan and the first fifteen years of my life.

My mother pulls me to her, speaking softly of my aunt in North Carolina, how much she'd love my company, how beautiful the South is.

———————•———————

How do I stop this?

Birthing stools.

I try to imagine Caryn sitting in one of those birthing stools, like the pained, strained woman in the picture. I close the book. I close my eyes.

I do that a great deal as I struggle through. When I cannot take it, I close my eyes, and I am closing them at many things. But then I shut tight and can see Caryn herself—lying on her side with a pillow between her knees, or with a giant amniocentesis needle harpooning her exposed round belly—and my eyes snap open again and I am sweating.

I clutch at my stomach, twist uncomfortably on the bed. There is no comfortable position for this.

But I go on. I feel like I am walking up the sheer face of a mountain. My legs are weak, I am disoriented. I want to quit, I don't know where I'm going or what I am going to do when I get there.

But I am climbing, goddamnit. Because it is there.

Some psychotic monster is trying out positions, in a chapter on sex during pregnancy. Sex.

During pregnancy.

I feel like rescuing her. I feel like kicking his ass right off the page.

I cannot imagine.

So much of this, I cannot imagine.

Time is passing, and I am climbing. Chapter after chapter, and all the way into the unknowns of the woman's body and the fetus and the night. I don't stop. I nearly stop. I want to stop at the labor pictures but I can't and I very very nearly stop at the afterbirth section, on something called lochia, which the book says is going to leak out of mother Caryn long after the cheering stops.

I don't stop at anything, though. Not even the dawn.

Light is coming through my window when I make my way through the huge "further reading" section and the frightening, packed, "in case of problems" section.

"'In case of problems,'" I read out loud. There's a joke. I am now well-read on the subject.

Mistake. I never should have opened the damn thing.

Mistake. I should have read it a long time ago. Three lifetimes ago.

In case of problems.

I know it all now. I am panicked. And guilty as hell.

How could I do this to anybody?

I turn the last page. To a big expanse of blank paper, with a tiny black-and-white photo of a sort of fruit seller's scale, with a white porcelain bowl settled on top. Cradling a shiny bawling baby, alone at the center of a vast, clean, cold emptiness.

Seven pounds, seven ounces.

I jump off the bed, grab my coat.

———•———

The night air is cool. I lean out the window of our car, feeling it against my face. In the back, Delia is singing a song about how crazy love is. She is off-key and emphasizing certain words. "You make me DRIVE and DRIVE and DRIVE," she sings. "You DRIVE me crazy. You make me LOOK and LOOK and LOOK for you. I'm LOOKING crazy . . ." until Mama tells her to stop acting the fool. After that, the car is quiet. It's a long drive to North Carolina. Mama and Delia will stay a week. Maybe I'll stay for always. Boston grows smaller and smaller behind us.

———————•———————

The Charger is right up on the sidewalk. I sit inside for the first hour flipping pages, staring up at Caryn's window, flipping pages. The photos and drawings are becoming burned like laser images into my brain. Swelling bellies, side views of upside-down bulb-headed babies fitted just so perfectly inside mama.

I spend the second hour reading, on the hood of the car. Health of mother and child. Exercise, nutrition, childbirth options. The role of the father.

The city is waking up. I hear the click of heels, the swish of skirts as people pass me by. The chug of car engines behind me. I am aware of being stared at, but I can't see anybody. I see the book. I see the window.

By nine o'clock I am sitting on Caryn's steps.

By ten I am standing in the doorway, ringing the bell.

There are three guys sitting on my father's Charger.

Caryn and I are going to read this book together.

It has to be. It can't not be.

I will wait right here, until it is.

A Note From the Authors

The idea for "The Rialto" came about when the two of us were teaching together at Vermont College. We found, through working together and comparing notes, histories, opinions, that we were remarkably similar people in a lot of ways. More compatible than two solitary writers tend to be.

But it wasn't until sometime later, in a long-distance phone conversation—very long-distance because Chris was living in Ireland and Jackie was living in Brooklyn—that we broached the subject. "Ever feel like collaborating?" somebody asked. "I was thinking about that myself," somebody replied.

It simply made too much sense. The two of us had by then carved out our distinctly different niches in fiction. What would happen if we tried to bring them together?

We were to find out. The characters, and their creators, began a years-long tango, embracing one another, repelling one another. Months of intense interaction would be followed by months of obstinate silence. Undeniable similarities challenged by seemingly irreconcilable differences. Like a trick we were playing on ourselves, we were being forced to work out issues of our characters.

It all became much trickier than we imagined. Quitting was just as hard as sticking with it, and neither option completely solved everything.

In the end, the story was as organic as we could make it. The characters had fought it out, played it out, and were left to confront a result that was even more challenging than what they had started out with.

"The Rialto" is excerpted from a novel-in-progress.

ENCHANTED NIGHT

JAMES HOWE

Mariah lay crushed under the oppressive weight of the present. The past had been wiped away, the future made meaningless, by the words, *Your father is dead.*

Time passed without her. From her bedroom she could hear the buzz of voices beneath her. Her grandmother's, her uncle's, Aaron's, and Dee's. From time to time, her mother came into her room and asked, "How are you doing?" Mariah answered in a voice that came from somewhere outside her body. She didn't understand how her mother could do it. Keep going. How she could sit in the armchair in the living room below and drink her grandmother's tea and wait for the rabbi and get the words *cemetery* and *coffin* and *sitting shiva* past her lips.

She wrapped herself in her white down comforter and welcomed oblivion.

Late in the afternoon, her mother lay down beside her and held her so tightly she thought she would break, and the two of them began to sob and didn't stop for twenty minutes. It was their sobbing that kept them from shattering into a million pieces.

The room grew dark. Mariah's mother whispered, "How did this happen?"

The past flickered in the darkness as Mariah remembered asking the same question a week earlier when Danny had broken up with her.

"You just can't make a commitment, Mariah. You want a little of *everything* . . ."

"What's wrong with *that?*"

"Nothing, except when one of the 'things' you want a little of is a person. You know, like a living, breathing human being. Like *me.*"

"God, Danny, you're so dramatic. I swear, sometimes I think *you're* the girl in this relationship."

"Lucky for you I'm smart enough not to take that as an insult."

"Anyway, I don't see your point."

"You don't want to see my point, Mariah. It's like with the flute."

"Oh, please, don't start with that."

"Well, you won't listen to your parents. I used to think you'd listen to me. You're so good, Mariah. You know you are. You could be playing with the Civic. But you won't take it seriously. Well, I feel like your flute sometimes. No crude jokes intended."

Mariah laughed. God, she loved Danny. The way he made her laugh. The way he cared so much. She touched his cheek and said, "I'm sorry. I'll try to be better."

Danny shook his head. "No, no, you won't. You say things like that all the time. They're just words, M. They don't mean anything. Look, I'm tired of being just another thing you fit into your busy schedule. I'm tired of the way you skim the surface of life, you know? I can't hack it anymore."

Mariah took her hand away. She held her breath.

"You could be so good at *us*, M. You could be so good, but you just don't want to put in the time. I'm sorry . . . I . . ."

Danny turned away.

"I don't want us to see each other anymore," he said.

That all happened when Mariah was a child. Now she was sixteen and ancient and everything that had happened up until her father's death belonged to the child she was no more. Even Danny. Even what only a week before she had absurdly thought of as a broken heart.

Dee was sitting on the edge of her bed, cradling a cup of soup. "Won't you eat something, sweetheart?"

Why did people always think that food was the answer to everything?

Mariah lay on her back, looking up at the phosphorescent stars her father had put on her ceiling when she was nine. She gazed at the constellations as she did almost every night before falling asleep and she thought, *They're all there. Every single plastic star is still up there, clinging to the ceiling, and my father . . . Dad . . . Daddy . . . is gone.*

"It doesn't make sense," she said, her voice hoarse from not having spoken in such a long time.

"No," Dee agreed, putting the cup down on the night table.

Mariah looked up into Dee's face. Aaron and Dee had been her parents' best friends forever. She'd known this face since she was a baby. She'd known it as the lines had grown around the eyes and mouth and the color of the hair surrounding it had changed, subtly. But it was the same face, always—wide and expansive, the kindest, the most loving face Mariah had ever seen. Eyes that invited you in, like candlelit windows on a wintry night. Mariah thought, *If I look long enough into Dee's eyes, I'll be swallowed up.*

And that would be good. To be swallowed up. To disappear.

"I want to die," she told Dee.

"Oh, no, no," Dee crooned, leaning forward with open arms.

"I do. I want to go find Daddy."

Dee froze, and, as if it had been punched, her face collapsed and the tears came before she could do anything to stop them.

Mariah sat up, folding Dee into her arms.

From downstairs she could hear the murmur of voices. She thought of the family and friends and neighbors who had gathered around her and her mother as soon as they'd heard the news. And the truth came to her, gently, simply: They were all missing him. They were all hurting. There were no adults, no children. Just hearts that ached and minds that were swimming in the same pool of confusion. Perhaps they all felt as she did, wanting to disappear, wanting to find Daddy.

• • •

". . . nineteen, twenty. Ready or not, here I come!"

Mariah puffed out her cheeks, holding her breath to keep herself from giggling. She had discovered the perfect hiding spot. Daddy would never find her here.

"I'm going to get you, little chipmunk," her father's voice sang out. "And when I get you, I'm going to *tickle* you!"

No fair! Mariah wanted to shout. Tickling wasn't allowed, and her father knew it. But then she thought, *He's tricking me! He* wants *me to shout. Well, I'll show him!*

She clamped her lips shut and waited. But as the minutes passed and the shadows outside the trellised crawl space grew longer, Mariah began to worry he'd never find her.

"Mariah!" her father called out. "Mariah, where are you?"

I'm here! Mariah thought. She was shivering.

"Mariah! The game's over! You win. Where *are* you? Mariah!"

Say it, Mariah thought. *Say you won't tickle me.*

Her father's legs crisscrossed past her perfect hiding place.

"Mariah, I mean it now! Come out from where you're hiding! Are you hurt? Mariah, answer me!"

"I win!" Mariah declared, popping out from under the porch just as her father had passed her for the sixth or seventh time. Her joy turned quickly to tears as she saw the angry look on his face.

"Mariah, you could have been hurt! How did you get under there? Why didn't you answer me?"

"I didn't want . . ."

"What?"

"I didn't want you to tickle me."

Her father's anger vanished in an instant. He knelt down and took her in his arms. "Oh, Mariah, I wouldn't have tickled you."

"But you said—"

"I was just teasing. I won't do it again, I promise. But you have to promise me something, too. Promise me you won't disappear like that. I got scared something had happened to you."

"But it's hide-and-seek. You were supposed to find me."

"I know, I know. And I will always *try* to find you, Mariah. But if I can't, then you have to find me. Okay? Understood?"

Mariah nodded into her father's shoulder. Patting him on the back, she said, "Don't worry, Daddy, we'll always find each other."

Her tears gone, she said, "My turn."

"No, no more hide-and-seek right now. Let's go inside and make some lemonade, what do you say?"

Mariah put her hand into her father's, and they walked into the house.

Mariah was four. Her father would live forever.

Danny's face was almost as pale as the milk he was slowly pouring into his coffee.

Mariah sat across from him at the breakfast room table. Outside in the dark was the lawn where she had once played hide-and-seek with her father.

She sipped her coffee, barely tasting it. But the warmth felt good.

"I'm glad you're here," she told Danny.

"Me, too," Danny said. He left his coffee sitting on the table, spoke to it haltingly.

"Your dad . . . he was such a cool guy. Geez, I . . . I can't believe I'm saying *was*. This is too weird. I mean, just this morning . . ." He stopped addressing the mug, looked out the blackened window, glanced at Mariah out of the corner of his eye, then bent down to tie or retie the laces in his running shoes.

The sound of other voices drifting in from other rooms carried them both through the next few minutes.

When he lifted his head, Danny's face looked as if it had been clawed. He wiped his nose on his sleeve. "So are you going to do it?" he asked.

"Do what? Oh, that. God, no. How could you even think?"

"Your dad would love . . . would have loved it, M. You know he would."

Mariah sighed. She was doing a lot of that suddenly, sighing. "My grandmother's crazy, okay? I know she wants it to be a nice funeral, but it's not like it's my bat mitzvah or something. She just wants to show off."

"M!"

"Oh, bad me. But you know what my grandmother's like, always needing everything to be beautiful and, I don't know, proper. She's like the original Jewish Martha Stewart. Well, excuse me for saying so, but this isn't exactly the moment to be worrying about beautiful and proper, you know?"

Danny nodded.

"My dad loved hearing me play the flute. I know that. And I wish I could do it—not for Grandma's sake, but for his—I wish I could play at his funeral, but . . . I just . . . Look, I don't know how I'm going to get through tomorrow, okay, let alone get up in front of people and play my flute. The rabbi even asked me if I wanted to speak. Give me a break. I can't believe we're even talking about stuff like this. If I hear the word 'arrangements' one more time, I'm going to scream."

Mariah sighed. "This is *not* one of my favorite things about being Jewish."

Danny looked at her, puzzled.

"The funeral has to take place within twenty-four hours of the death. I mean, who's ready to deal with it? I'm afraid I'm going to fall apart. Totally."

Danny opened his mouth to speak, then stopped and said nothing.

"What?" Mariah asked.

He shook his head. Finally, he said, "You'll be okay. You've got your mom. At least, she understands about the flute thing."

"Mm. Lucky for me she didn't inherit the Martha Stewart gene."

Danny laughed, and, to her surprise, Mariah joined him. They both took sips of their coffee, then looked across the table at each other, shyly, as if they'd just met.

"I'm glad you're here," Mariah said again.

"Me, too," said Danny.

• • •

Listening to the sound of her mother breathing, Mariah thought, *Thank goodness, she's asleep at last.* She picked up the clock on her night table. Two-thirty. Putting it back with a sigh, she wondered when *her* sleeping pill would kick in.

She sat up and looked out the window. There was a full moon. *Great,* Mariah thought. *On top of everything else.* She could never get to sleep easily when there was a full moon. Now her mind began to wander, picking up speed as it went.

Her father saying goodbye to her that morning.

The rain.

The car hitting the pool of water, sliding over it like a marble on a sheet of glass until it hit the wall.

Her father . . . his body . . .

No, she wouldn't let herself imagine that.

The look on her mother's face when she told her the news.

The sudden emptiness in the pit of her stomach.

The world coming to an end.

Lying curled up on her bed all day.

Danny there, drinking coffee. The way he bent down to tie his laces.

His face.

How long had it been since he'd told her he didn't want to see her anymore? A week?

And before that . . .

She hadn't told him, hadn't told her father or mother, hadn't even told Mr. Carlson, that she had auditioned for the Civic Symphony the day before Danny had broken up with her. Had made a mess of it, been told, "Try again next year." Had left crying.

Had decided to give up the flute.

Hadn't told anyone.

Yet.

The one thing she was good at. But not good enough.

First that, then Danny ending it. Ending them.

And now . . .

Loss upon loss.

She looked down at her mother. Her mother, who couldn't bring herself to sleep in her own bed that night, *their* bed. Her mother, a widow.

A widow.

A chill went through her.

She looked back out the window, let her mind float until it took her back to the fourth grade. The time she'd started playing the flute. She had felt so grownup when she brought home that little black case and showed her father how to assemble the instrument inside, how to hold it just so, how to form your lips to make a sound come out.

"Do you want me to teach you?" she had asked him.

"Yes, please," he had replied as if she had asked if he'd like more tea.

And so for the rest of that year she had shared each lesson with him, taught him how to place his fingers, how to play a B-flat and, by the time of her first concert, how to play "Hot Cross Buns." He wasn't very good at it. Too much breath, too many notes that sounded like squeaky doors. She had laughed and said, "It's good you know how to do other things." And he had laughed and agreed.

He did know how to do other things. He was good at everything. At least, that's what Mariah had believed until she had started playing the flute. Everything she attempted to do, from drawing to Rollerblading to playing the piano, he did with ease.

"Here, let me show you something else you can do with that!" he would say enthusiastically about each new interest, taking each thing from her before she could even claim it as her own. She knew he didn't mean to, he just had so many interests, so many talents.

"Why aren't you drawing anymore?" he'd ask her.

"What happened to that story you were writing?"

"Don't you want to finish learning that duet?"

She'd just shrug in response to each question. She didn't have the words to think, much less say, "Because that story doesn't belong to me anymore. Because you can draw so much better than I can. Because while I fumble with the right hand of the duet, you're playing flourishes with the left hand, improvising and embellishing, not even noticing that my hands are shaking and there are tears in my eyes."

Mariah hugged the blankets to her.

How could she be thinking these things about her father?

And how could she give up the flute, the one thing he had not taken from her, the one thing that was hers?

Mariah remembered the dream she'd had when she was nine.

A flute is playing far away. I am in my bedroom. The music, beautiful and natural as a bird, calls to me.

I walk out of my room, down long halls, stairways.

I come into the dining room and there you are, standing in front of the wide expanse of windows looking out onto the yard. Your back is to me. There is a full moon and its light pours into the darkened room. You almost shimmer. I do not know it is you at first. I think it is some heavenly visitor. You turn your head slightly.

It is you.

Playing my flute.

The music is so beautiful, and it is you playing my flute.

You stop suddenly, turn to look at me as if I'm a ghost. You look down at the flute in your hands.

"Mariah."

I run away. Do you follow? I don't remember.

Sometime later—the next morning?—I tell you I am never going to play the flute again. You pick it up and awkwardly form your lips. You blow. The flute wheezes apologetically. "You see?" you say to me. "I can't play."

"But I heard you," I say.

You tell me, "Last night was enchanted. I picked up your flute and the music just poured through me. It was magical. But I'll never be able to play like that again."

I say, "I'll never be able to play like that at all."

You look sad and serious as you shake your head. "Don't say that. You'll play better than that, much better. And if you are ever as lucky as I was, to pick up the flute on a night that's enchanted, the music you make will be the music of angels."

Mariah couldn't remember how the dream ended. She remained a long time sitting up in bed, waiting for the clock downstairs to chime three, then four, waiting for sleep.

• • •

The day of the funeral felt like another dream. Somehow, she showered and dressed and found herself at the synagogue, where hands and faces pressed against her and mouths formed words. She nodded and sighed and twisted her hands and thought how ridiculous she must look, like a grieving widow in a bad movie. But it was her mother who was the widow. Her mother, who doubled over when Aaron stood in front of the large crowd and talked about all their years of friendship, the camping trips and barbecues and shared birthday celebrations.

Others spoke about her father's love of life, his boundless enthusiasm for every new thing that interested him. They talked of his love for Mariah and her mother, of his being a family man, a good Jew. No one spoke of his success in business, because it had never been his work that defined him.

Through it all, Mariah held her mother's hands. She turned from time to time to look over her shoulder at Danny, whose sad sweet smile seemed always to be waiting for her. She felt her lips quiver and squeezed her eyes shut and prayed that the day would end and prayed that the day would never end because when it did life was going to turn real. And reality no longer included her father.

Somehow, the funeral was over and they were at the cemetery and, somehow, they were lowering her father's body into the ground and, somehow, she was standing with a shovel in her hands scooping up dirt and flinging it over her father's coffin, and the sound it made was not the music of angels. It was harsh and dry and unbearably final.

Before they left the cemetery, Mariah stood alone at her father's grave.

"I'm sorry I couldn't play the flute for you," she told him. She waited, for what she did not know, and listened to the wind rustling leaves in a nearby tree and an airplane rumbling in the distance. She thought about the people inside the plane, eating peanuts and reading magazines, on their way from one place to another, and she said a quick prayer wishing them safely to their destination, and she looked down at the earth and said again, "I'm sorry, Daddy. I'm sorry I couldn't play my flute for you."

Danny called Mariah every day for weeks after her father's death, to ask how she was doing, to let her know he was there if she needed him. Finally, she said, "You have a funny way of breaking up with people."

He said, "Ouch."

She said, "I'm sorry."

He said, "It's okay."

She wanted to say, "I love you so much, can we try again?" But she didn't.

He said, "See you at school tomorrow."

She said, "Yeah."

He said, "Do you want me to stop calling you?"

She said, "No."

He said, "Good."

They said goodbye, and Mariah went into the kitchen and made her mother a cup of tea.

• • •

Mariah waited until the end of the semester to tell Mr. Carlson she wasn't going to continue with the flute. But when she went to talk with him, he surprised her by saying, "I'd like to feature you in the spring concert, Mariah. Here, look at these three pieces and let me know which you find the most challenging."

"Challenging?" Mariah said.

Mr. Carlson laughed. "What do you want me to do? Give you a piece you can play in your sleep? A musician like you? Come on, Mariah, you know me better than that. So look them over, let me know what you think by next week."

Mariah looked down at the music he had handed her. Debussy, Massenet, Grieg. They were all pieces for flute and orchestra. Mr. Carlson had never featured an individual musician before, never given anyone more than a small solo spot.

"But why?" Mariah asked.

Mr. Carlson regarded Mariah solemnly. "Don't you know how extraordinarily gifted you are? I don't get musicians of your caliber very often, Mariah. When I do, I want to help them grow. And I want to share the wealth."

"It's not because . . ." Mariah didn't know how to get the words out.

At first, he didn't understand. And then he did. "No, this is not a sympathy move, Mariah. Do you think I'd really give you a solo in a concert to try to make up for your dad's death somehow? You've got to trust me on this one. You are very, very good, and it's time you had the chance to play up to your own standards."

Mariah left, holding the music against her heart. She had forgotten why she had gone to talk to Mr. Carlson. Now all she could think was, *I'll never be able to play any of these pieces.*

But in her bedroom that evening, she tried the Massenet and found it not easy, but a piece she was certain she could manage with work. Besides, it had always been one of her favorites. She put aside the Grieg, which she didn't know, and the Debussy, which she thought might be considered a cliché, and began working her way through the Massenet again.

Her mother came to her room and leaned against the door frame, listening.

When Mariah put down the flute, her mother said, "Your father . . ."

"I know, I know," said Mariah. "My father loved to hear me play."

"No," said her mother. "Not that."

"What, then?"

Mariah's mother shook her head as if there was something she wanted to say but couldn't, then came into the room and took Mariah into her arms. "Your father loved you," she said. "That's all."

But that wasn't all. It was on a night when the moon was full that Mariah discovered the rest.

Hide-and-seek. She was It.

Mariah lay sleepless on her bed, looking up at the glowing stars and planets above her, remembering how her father had brought them home for her the same day she had announced an interest in astrology. Had named all of the constellations as he tacked them up on her ceiling, almost falling off the ladder in his insistence on exactitude. Even so, the Big Dipper was more than a little off, and that had always been a joke between them.

For some reason, Mariah started thinking about the piece she was going to be playing in a few weeks at the spring concert. There was one section she just couldn't get. No matter how much Mr. Carlson worked with her, she couldn't seem to master it. Mariah thought about how up until this year she had imagined herself becoming a concert flutist. Now, the idea seemed like a bad joke. With all the talent everyone kept telling her she possessed, she hadn't even been good enough to get into the Civic. Mr. Carlson's trusting her to play a demanding solo piece suddenly seemed cruel.

She would tell him she couldn't do it. He couldn't *make* her, after all. So what if she was letting him down? Better that than making a total fool of herself.

Mariah could see the moon out of her window. She had stopped taking pills to help her sleep and she worried about her mother's reliance on them. Still, she wondered if she should sneak into her mother's bathroom and take one. It was late and she had an important test the next day.

Moving by her sleeping mother, she passed through the large walk-in closet that led to her parents' bathroom and, as quietly as she could, opened the medicine cabinet, found the bottle of pills, and tipped one into her open palm.

On her way back through the closet, she stopped and

let her fingers gingerly touch her father's shirts and jackets and folded-over pants. She pressed her face into his clothes, inhaled the fading aroma of her father's skin, wondered how often her mother did this, wondered how long before her mother would finally have the strength to empty the closet out. Feeling her father's presence in his clothes, she could imagine how hard it would be for her mother to remove them. She remembered how her mother had insisted on using Mariah's bathroom for several weeks after her father died. How upset she had been when she had heard Mariah running water in the sink of the master bathroom. She had burst in on her, screaming, "How dare you use my bathroom! Get out! Get out!" Mariah had fled, angry and confused. It wasn't until the next morning, as she was packing Mariah's lunch, that her mother had said, "There were hairs in the sink. They were all I had left of him."

How do you ever say goodbye? Mariah wondered. *How do you ever let go?*

Looking up, she noticed a hat of her father's on a high shelf. She remembered how he'd worn it for years when she was little. It was a silly hat, really. A sort of cowboy thing with a wide band made of ostrich feathers or some such. But she had loved it, and she suspected now that he had kept wearing it for her sake long after he'd grown tired of it. If she stood on tiptoe, she could just reach its brim with her outstretched fingers.

As the hat tumbled to the floor, Mariah saw that she had pulled something else with it. A box of some kind was hanging precariously over the shelf's edge. She attempted to push it back into its place, but there was something so familiar about the feel of it that she grew curious and carefully pulled it down. As the hat had tugged at the box, the box now tugged at something else—papers—that flew to the floor and scattered about her feet. But Mariah didn't pay any notice of them. She was too stunned by the box, too full of confusion at the mystery of it.

What she held in her hands was a case for a flute, and she felt with certainty that the flute inside had been her father's.

With trembling hands she picked up the fallen papers and carried them all downstairs with her. Turning on a light in the dining room, she opened the case and beheld her father's flute. It was much like her old one, nothing grand or special, a student's flute. She took it out, assembled it, lifted it to her lips—and then caught sight of one of the pieces of sheet music that had fallen from the shelf. It was Debussy's *Clair de lune*, one of the pieces Mr. Carlson had given her.

She opened its pages and began to play.

Tears filled her eyes. This was the music from her dream.

She continued, but her hands began shaking badly and her vision became so blurred she could no longer make out the notes. She lowered the flute and looked out into the yard, trying to understand.

"Don't stop."

She turned to see her mother standing in the doorway.

"My dream," Mariah said.

"Dream?" said her mother.

"This is just like my dream. Except you're me, and I'm . . . Daddy."

After she told her mother her dream, her mother said, "But that really happened. Don't you remember?"

"But I thought Daddy couldn't play the flute. I *must* have dreamed it."

"Daddy played the flute beautifully," Mariah's mother told her. "And he loved it. But that night . . ."

"Enchanted night," said Mariah. "That's what we called it."

"Yes." Mariah's mother pulled back a chair from the dining room table and sat. Mariah remained standing in front of the window, the light of the moon bathing her shoulders, the back of her head.

"Your father was devastated that night. He came into the bedroom after he'd gotten you back to sleep and just cried and cried. It was his crying that woke me."

"Why?" Mariah asked. "What did he have to cry about?"

"He said to me, 'I just keep taking things away from her. I keep robbing her of herself.' He didn't mean to, sweetie. He just loved that you were like him, gifted in so many ways. He couldn't help wanting to share all that with you.

"He hadn't intended to let you know how well he played. But you know what your father was like, he could never contain his enthusiasm for long. I guess he couldn't sleep that night—like you, he was always restless on moonlit nights—so he must have been wandering around downstairs, seen your flute, and couldn't stop himself from playing."

"*Clair de lune,*" Mariah said. "How fitting."

Her mother laughed. "It was his favorite. Besides, you know how dramatic and sentimental he could be. Full moon. Flute. It was too much for him to resist."

Mariah sat down opposite her mother. "So I really don't have anything that's just mine," she said.

"Oh, no," her mother said, reaching her hand across the table to grasp Mariah's. "That's not true. You're like your father in so many ways. You're both jacks-of-all-trades. But your father was master of none. He never had the singular gift that you have. You are by far the better musician. He knew that, and that's why he put his flute away and never played again. He wanted to make room for you, don't you see? He wanted you to be able to develop your talent, not hop, skip, and jump the way he did."

"Is it bad we're talking about Daddy like this?" Mariah asked.

"He wasn't a saint. And his dying didn't turn him into one."

Mariah traced her mother's fingers with her own. "You know what I wish?" she said.

"What?"

"I wish I could play this piece instead of the Massenet for the concert."

"Well, why don't you ask? Maybe it's not too late."

"Danny?"

"Oh, hey M, what's up?"

"I need to ask you something. I hope it's not too late."

"What?"

"I . . . I just want to know if . . . if we can . . . can we try again? Us? Can we try that again?"

"I'd really like that," Danny said.

"Me, too," said Mariah.

Mariah played Debussy's *Clair de lune* at the spring concert. Mr. Carlson agreed to the change, as long as she would work on the Massenet as an audition piece for the Civic. Mariah said she would.

When she stepped out in front of the orchestra to play that night, she closed her eyes for the smallest moment and pictured herself standing in front of her dining room window looking out into a moonlit night. She thought, *Shall I begin?* And she heard him say, *Yes, please*, as if she had asked if he'd like more tea. She opened her eyes and announced, "This is for my father."

She raised the flute to her lips.

It was an enchanted night, and the music she made was the music of angels.

A Note From the Author

Like so many pieces of writing, "Enchanted Night" has several points of origin. The earliest goes back to when my daughter was very young and I became aware of how I could easily overpower her enthusiasm for a new interest with my own eagerness. I worried, rightly so, that I was robbing her of something by being too interested or too ready to share my own talents and knowledge. I pulled back, and—writer that I am—jotted down my first notes for this story.

When my daughter was eight, she and I were in a car accident together. The experience had a profound impact on us both and I knew I would have to write about it someday. And then, less than two years later, my marriage ended.

When I began working on this story I didn't know I would be writing out of the pain and soul-searching engendered by the accident and end of my marriage. What I did know was that in essence this was a story about my daughter and me—about her growing up and finding her own way, about my trying to give her the space she needs to be her own person, about the losses

and near losses that have colored our lives together

and apart, and about the love that binds us and enables

us to find each other even when one of us is lost.

AUTHOR BIOGRAPHIES

SUMMER OF LOVE
ANNETTE CURTIS KLAUSE

Annette Curtis Klause was born in Bristol, England, in 1953. When she was fifteen, she moved to the United States with her family and lived in Washington, D.C. She has a B.A. and an MLS from the University of Maryland in College Park, and now heads the children's department of a busy suburban public library in Montgomery County, Maryland. She likes to write about unusual people such as vampires, werewolves, and aliens; the book she's writing currently has characters much stranger than that. Her published novels are *The Silver Kiss* (Delacorte, 1990, Dell, 1992), *Alien Secrets* (Delacorte, 1993; Dell, 1995), and *Blood and Chocolate* (Delacorte, 1997; Dell, 1999). Annette and her husband have had eleven cats together. Today they live in Hyattsville, Maryland, with the latest three—Lirazel, Esmé, and Mr. Tod.

WHAT ARE YOU GOOD AT?
RODERICK TOWNLEY

Roderick Townley has always had a hard time sticking to one kind of writing. The sorry truth is that he has never really tried. For a long while he thought of himself as a poet, until he looked around and noticed, besides his two slim volumes of verse, a couple of novels, several works of nonfiction, and some books of literary criticism. Mr. Townley's favorite books are his most recent: an anthology of essays called *Night Errands: How Poets Use Dreams*, and a middle-grade novel called *The Great Good Thing*. He lives in Kansas, has two children (Jesse and Grace), and is married to poet Wyatt Townley.

Atomic Blues Pieces
Angela Johnson

Born in Tuskegee, Alabama, Angela Johnson moved with her family to Ohio when she was two. She has lived in Ohio ever since, but family ties to Alabama remain strong and inspire her writing. She has written over twenty-five books for children and young adults. Among her most recent picture books are *The Wedding* and *The Winding Road*. Her novels include *Toning the Sweep* and *Heaven*. She is also the author of *Gone from Home*, a collection of short stories, and *The Other Side*, a volume of poetry. Her numerous awards include the Ezra Jack Keats Award, two Coretta Scott King Awards, and the Lee Bennett Hopkins Poetry Award.

The Tin Butterfly
Norma Fox Mazer

Norma Fox Mazer is the author of two short story collections and twenty-five novels, for which she has received numerous awards, including the California Young Reader's Medal, two Iowa Teen Awards, an Edgar, two Lewis Carroll Shelf Awards, the Christopher Award, a National Book Award nomination, and a Newbery Honor. She has also coedited a collection of women's poetry, contributed articles to many journals, and written original short stories for close to a dozen anthologies. Her most recent book is *Goodnight, Maman*.

THE FIRE POND

MICHAEL J. ROSEN

Michael J. Rosen's fiction for young readers includes a chapter book, *The Blessing of the Animals*, and a collection of five stories, *The Heart Is Big Enough*, which received the Ohioana Library Book Award. Among his many other books for children are *A School for Pompey Walker*, winner of the inaugural Museum of Tolerance Once Upon a World Book Award, and *Elijah's Angel*, winner of the National Jewish Book Award. He has edited, illustrated, or written several books to benefit Share Our Strength's anti-hunger initiatives and The Company of Animals Fund, a granting program he founded to support humane efforts across the country. His books for adults include three volumes of poetry, and various anthologies, including *Dog People*, *Horse People*, and *Mirth of the Nation*, a contemporary humor biennial.

Rosen serves as a literary adviser to The Thurber House, a cultural center in James Thurber's restored home, where he has worked since its inception, and often works with teachers and children as a visiting author. He lives in central Ohio.

CHAIR: A STORY FOR VOICES

VIRGINIA EUWER WOLFF

Virginia Euwer Wolff's novels have all been selected as ALA Best Books for Young Adults or ALA Notable Books for Young Readers, sometimes both. Among her prizes are the International Reading Association Award (for *Probably Still Nick Swansen*); the Janusz Korczak Book Award Honor from the Anti-Defamation League (for *The Mozart Season*); the Golden Kite, the Bank Street Prize, and the *Booklist* Top of the List (for *Make Lemonade*); and the Jane Addams Award for the Women's International League for Peace and Freedom (for *Bat 6*). Her new book is *True Believer*, a sequel to *Make Lemonade*. She lives in Oregon.

RED SEVEN

C. B. CHRISTIANSEN

For Cathy Christiansen, stories are as necessary as family, friends, food. She says, "Sometimes there's a story I'm longing to hear and I make movie or book selections from my 'highly recommended' list and I'm still not satisfied. I realize, then, the story I'm longing to hear is the one I'm supposed to be writing." Ms. Christiansen is the author of six books for children and young adults. Her latest novel, *I See the Moon*, is an ALA Best Book for Young Adults, ALA Notable Book, ALA Quick Pick for

Reluctant Readers, Notable Trade Book in the Language Arts and in the Field of Social Studies, and a Bank Street College Book of the Year.

Christiansen currently writes novels and screenplays from her home in Medina, Washington.

SHOOFLY PIE
NAOMI SHIHAB NYE

Naomi Shihab Nye's books include *Fuel* (poems), *Habibi* (a novel for teens that won five Best Book Awards), and *Never in a Hurry* (essays). She has edited six prize-winning anthologies of poetry for young readers, including *This Same Sky*, *The Tree Is Older than You Are*, *The Space Between our Footsteps: Poems and Paintings from the Middle East*, *What Have You Lost?* and *Salting the Ocean: 100 Poems by Young Poets*. She lives in downtown San Antonio, Texas, a block from the river, with her husband, photographer Michael Nye, and their son, Madison.

YOU'RE NOT A WINNER
UNLESS YOUR PICTURE'S IN THE PAPER
AVI

Avi's many award-winning books for young readers include the Newbery Honor Books *Nothing but the Truth* and *The True Confessions of Charlotte Doyle*, as well as the series Tales from Dimwood Forest, which includes *Poppy*, winner of the *Boston Globe–Horn Book* Award. His many other books include tales of mystery and fantasy, short stories, and historical fiction for young readers. He is the founder of Breakfast Serials, the public charity that provides books for kids to the nation's newspapers. He lives with his family in Denver, Colorado.

SEASON'S END

WALTER DEAN MYERS

Walter Dean Myers was born in Martinsburg, West Virginia, but was brought to Harlem by his foster parents at age three. He was brought up there and went to school there. As a kid there were never enough gloves to go around and never enough balls in good enough condition to play much serious baseball. He attended Stuyvesant High School until the age of seventeen when he joined the army.

Army service included time spent as a radio technician and playing basketball. After serving four years in the army, he worked at various jobs including the U.S. Post Office, the Employment service, and finally as a senior editor for Bobbs-Merrill Publishing. He has also earned a B.A. from Empire State College.

Walter has been writing since childhood and publishing since 1969 when he won the Council on Interracial Books for Children contest which resulted in the publication of his first book for children, *Where Does the Day Go?*, published by *Parent's* Magazine Press. Since then he has published sixty-five books for children and young adults. He has been awarded many times for his work in the field, including the Coretta Scott King Award five times. Two of his books were awarded Newbery Honors.

He has been awarded the Margaret A. Edwards Award and the Virginia Hamilton Award. For one of his latest books, *Monster*, he has received the first Michael Printz Award for Young Adult Literature awarded by the American Library Association. The book was also nominated a National Book Award Finalist.

THE RIALTO

JACQUELINE WOODSON AND CHRIS LYNCH

Jacqueline Woodson is the author of a number of books for children and young adults, including *The Other Side*, *From the Notebooks of Melanin Sun*, *If You Come Softly*, *I Hadn't Meant to Tell You This*, and *Miracle Boys*, winner of the Coretta Scott King Author Award.She has twice received the Coretta Scott King Honor Award and the Jane Addams Peace Award Honor, as well as a number of ALA Best Book Awards. Currently living in Brooklyn, New York, Jacqueline keeps in touch daily with Chris Lynch (who lives in Scotland) via phone and E-mail.

Chris Lynch was born in Boston and currently lives in Scotland. He is the author of several young adult novels, including *Slot Machine* and *Gypsy Davey*, and, most recently, *Extreme Elvin*, *Whitechurch*, *Gold Dust*, and *Freewill*.

ENCHANTED NIGHT

JAMES HOWE

James Howe is the author of the young adult novel *The Watcher*, a psychological study of four young people on a summer beach, which *The New York Times* called "a brave, dark, remarkable new novel." *The Watcher* was a real departure for Howe, who is best known for his humorous and entertaining novels for middle-grade readers, most notably the award-winning and highly popular Bunnicula series. The author of over seventy books for young readers, Howe has written—in addition to the Sebastian Barth mysteries and other books for middle-grade readers—a chapter book series about two best friends named Pinky and Rex, and numerous picture books, including *Horace and Morris but Mostly Dolores* and *I Wish I Were a Butterfly*. His newest book is *The Misfits*, a novel.

POWERFUL FICTION FROM
AWARD-WINNING AUTHOR
JAMES HOWE

"A knockout, one of the best of the year."
—*San Francisco Chronicle*

THE MISFITS
0-689-83955-3 (hardcover)
0-689-83956-1 (paperback)

THE WATCHER
0-689-80186-6 (hardcover)
0-689-82662-1 (trade paperback)
0-689-83533-7 (rack)
An ALA Quick Pick for Young Adults
An ALA Best Book for Young Adults

Edited by James Howe
THE COLOR OF ABSENCE
0-689-82862-4 (hardcover)
0-689-85667-9 (paperback)

Aladdin Paperbacks/Simon Pulse
Simon & Schuster Children's Publishing
www.SimonSays.com

Read Cynthia Voigt's acclaimed Tillerman cycle
from beginning to end:

HOMECOMING
"An enthralling journey to a gratifying end."
—*New York Times Book Review*

DICEY'S SONG
Winner of the Newbery Medal

A SOLITARY BLUE
A Newbery Honor Book

THE RUNNER

COME A STRANGER

SONS FROM AFAR

SEVENTEEN AGAINST THE DEALER